Mum,
For
reading
good !

WriteTime Anthology

TWO

Short Stories by Older Writers

TWO

Short Stories by Older Writers

Printed and bound in Great Britain by
Gemini Print Ltd
Shoreham-by-Sea, West Sussex

Edited by Irene Reed and Susan Twell
Designed by Tim Gwyther and Arron Wakeling
Lead Reader Nadia Mitchell

First Published 2021 by Shoreham Press CIC

ISBN Number 978-1-3999-0759-0

For details on WriteTime competitions and publications write to:
WriteTime, PO Box 2206, Shoreham-by-Sea, BN43 9FU, UK

info@writetime.org   www.writetime.org

This book is dedicated to all
key workers across the world.

Contents

Foreword

Welcome to WriteTime TWO. We are proud and excited to publish this second collection of short stories by older writers.

In its four short years WriteTime has become an important platform for writers here in the UK and around the world. What we all share is a love of the English language – its flexibility, its openness to new cultures and meanings.

The 36 stories here have been selected from the many hundreds submitted to our regular competitions over the past two years.

You will find some shockingly-clear observations of life. There are stories full of sensitivity and tenderness. There are the oddly offbeat and the frankly sinister too; and of course, representations of life during lockdown.

Just as you would expect from the growing WriteTime family of writers, readers and editors. Every one of us aged over 60 years. Each of us looking for the next story to tell.

We hope you enjoy the journey!

Hands
By Michael Dixon

Where is he? I look at my watch. He is 40 minutes late. The green stone in my ring reflects the flashing lights of the ride.

I'm leaning against the rails of the Waltzer waiting for Fran. I love fairgrounds. I love the smells of diesel, fried onions, sweet candyfloss and toffee apples, all mingled together. And I love the sounds, the wailing siren when a ride ends, the jingly tunes as the horses bob up and down on metal poles, the children giggling, looking for their parents and waving, as I did, with mum and dad waving back and smiling.

The boy on the Waltzer moves easily around the cars, untroubled by the undulation of the floor. He stops at a car with three teenage girls in and waits until it's slowing then spins it.

The girls scream, half in fear, half with excitement. The

fairground boy is not much older than the girls, about my age. I notice his hands grabbing the cab. LOVE is tattooed on the fingers of his right hand, HATE on the left.

My hands are long and slim. People comment on them, especially when I have the nails varnished. I raise the left one to examine the ring again. Fran will be here soon. He said he would.

I'm wearing a fringed suede skirt and matching bolero waistcoat. Fran likes it. He says it makes me look like a Western cowgirl. My blouse is pure white, the first two buttons undone.

The blinking lights of the Waltzer dance in the small green stone when I hold it to my face. Fran won the ring last week, the first night the fair was here. Won it on the shooting range and placed it on my finger. Fran has nice hands. We drove out on his motorbike and parked on the mountainside. He asked me if he was my first. I lied and said he was. They all want to know they're the first.

Someone taps me on the shoulder. I turn and see a boy from the alleys. One of them. They were hungry to learn, timid with their caresses and kisses. They waited for their turn. "You're next," I'd say and one would step forward, impatient for his few minutes.

"Hi, Joannie."

That's all he said. He moved from one leg to the other and stared at the slatted floor. I gave him a smile. It costs nothing.

"So, what are you doing?"

"I'm waiting for someone."

"Oh." He hesitated then said, "Perhaps me and the boys will see you one evening – you know, usual place." He licked his lips. "Well, see you then."

And he was gone. I couldn't remember his name. So many boys, cheap cider and fumbling hands. But no more of that. I'm with Fran now.

The ride finishes and the three girls leave the car, giggling, stumbling on jelly legs, glancing back at the fairground boy.

He watches them go, then, while the cars are filling up, approaches. There is a swagger about him, a confidence gained from so many girls in so many towns. He smiles. He has bad teeth.

"Hi there. Are you going to stand there all evening? Come on the Waltzer."

What if Fran comes and sees me with him spinning me around?

"I can't. I'm waiting for my boyfriend." He is my boyfriend. I have the ring and we sealed it on the mountain.

"Come on. It's free."

I shake my head. An angry shout. He turned. The man in the paybox beckons. The ride was starting. He grins, jumps onto the moving platform.

The klaxon sounds for the start of the ride, and the lights flash green, blue, red. He rides the platform like a surfer boy, stops at a car with three girls. They squeal in mock fright.

The ride ends and young men step off, giddy as drunken sailors, their girlfriends teetering on high heels.

He comes over again. "Come on. It'll only take a minute."

I think, why not, and follow him to a car, sit down and hold the bar tightly. It starts slowly, the car rotating left then right. The boy appears. LOVE touches my hair briefly before joining HATE to fling the car around.

My thoughts were spinning faster than the Waltzer but they were unwelcome. Why are thoughts so uncontrollable? They just come uninvited and mess up your head. I want good thoughts – of me and Fran, in the heather looking up at the stars.

The ride ends and the boy helps me out of the car. I am unsteady. He leads me off the ride and I smile at him.

Again I look at my watch. Then I see his blonde hair above a generator by the coconut shy. His head bobs up and down and in a few minutes he emerges. He has a girl with him. She smiles slyly and holds onto his arm. Fran looks over. He sees me but there is no smile, no recognition. He turns and walks in the opposite direction. I watch him go, slide the ring from my finger and let it fall. I nudge it with my foot. It falls through the slats.

I don't cry. I'm not sure how long I stood there, dreamlike with unbidden thoughts.

A hand taps me on the shoulder. It's the Waltzer boy.

"I've got a couple of hours off. Want to come back to my place?"

I nod and follow him. Behind the row of stalls – hoopla, roll-a-penny, coconut shy – are the caravans. He unlocks one and stands aside for me to enter.

In the corner is an unmade bed. I stand beside it and unbutton my blouse. He comes to me. His hand caresses my breast. It is the hand with the HATE tattoo. He kisses me roughly then pulls away to speak. I know what he will ask.

The Other Pianist
By David Allard

"Ya know, I always hated that Polanski movie, the horrible one with Ade Brody looking so miserable. It was kinda one note, ya know. I mean . . . OK, he survived, that is to say, his character survived while so many others perished, but really? Isn't life too short for such endooring sorrow?"

Schneider pauses and takes another sip of the 20-year-old malt, trying not to slurp. He places the drink on the bench within easy reach and lets his fingers move randomly, hovering a bare inch or two above the keyboard.

Schneider's suit is well worn, the seat of his pants shiny. A button on the left cuff hangs loose. He has a short-sleeved shirt beneath the suit but prefers not to expose his arms. He usually flips the tails of his jacket over the bench as he sits down, but this evening he has forgotten.

The blood-red light suffusing the Jerusalem YMCA opposite the hotel, saturating its beige stone, catches his eye through the picture window. He stops breathing for several seconds, mesmerised. If he steps outside now, the air will be magical – liquid and lightened by the sweet, sad smell of pine cones.

The street outside is quiet; the roar of evening traffic still to come.

"I am surprised, Stephen, that you watched the film, with your family history." It is a familiar, honeyed voice, with the faintest of accents.

Hakim always comes over for a chat at this time; the hotel dining-room is spick and span and ready for the evening meal, but the meal itself is an hour away.

The 20-year-old malt is his weekly gift to Schneider; a tribute to a different kind of loss to his own.

"Hakim, it's history. Where I come from, history is for celluloid, ya know?"

Hakim doesn't know, and raises an eyebrow. It is a useful device when faced with difficult diners, of which there are too many.

Schneider probably deserves better than that, as he never asks for anything.

"What? I never told ya? I'm a Californian. L.A., man. Home of Hollywood."

He plays a few chords and half-sings, half-chants:
All the leaves are brown
And the sky is grey

I went for a walk

On a winter's day . . .

His voice is croaky by the end of the stanza.

"Mr Schneider, do you still smoke so much?"

"Sure, why not. Hey, you only die once, Hakim. Don't you have any vices yourself?"

He does not wait for Hakim's answer; plays a few gentle, rippling chords and begins to sing again:

You only live twice, or so it seems

One life for yourself and one for your dreams.

He looks up at Hakim who is adjusting his bow-tie minutely. Hakim, as always, is impeccably dressed.

"Lemme repeat myself: don't you have any vices?"

Hakim gives Schneider his most charming smile.

"For myself, no, I can honestly say, but our people have always liked feuds, sometimes war." Hakim paused. "But your people? They have come to war recently, and love war greatly."

Schneider shrugs. "I guess you're right. Once you start dishing it out, instead of being on the receiving end, it gets to be a habit. We've always had feuds though. We call them family get-togethers. Friday night meals, Passover, whenever, whatever."

"Ah yes. A family gathering. That we share, for sure."

Stephen Schneider takes a burgundy dust cover from the top of the piano, and lays it reverently across the ivory keys. Getting up, he feels his knee joints crackle and winces. He checks the sofas and chairs scattered around low tables in the reception area.

"No-one yet, Hakim."

"The first couples will be along soon. Why do you always mention this, Mr Schneider?"

"Oh, I like to watch and imagine that it's my Deborah who is there and she is meeting someone nice, a good boy with a kind heart."

"Is that possible?"

Stephen Schneider shakes his head, and grins.

"Of course it's poss–i–ble," he said, dragging out the syllables. "The Almighty might intervene. That's possible, isn't it? No more of that Esalen bullshit."

"Of course." Hakim echoes, and grasps Schneider's wrist for a moment, calming the hand's tremor. "Pardon me for asking, but what is S L N, please?"

"Ach, California dreaming. Self-realisation. You shouldn't know from such an abomination. Navel-gazing."

Hakim looks away. He has no idea what Schneider means and wonders how quickly he can get away, while showing the due respect and courtesy the pianist deserves, however cranky he is becoming. He looks back when Schneider tugs on his sleeve.

"Hey, Hakim, lookie lookie. The first couple is arriving."

It is true. Carefully walking a few feet apart, two young Orthodox Jerusalemites have entered the hotel, in full public view.

"Ya know, it beats me." Schneider is speaking in a stage whisper now: "If the matchmaking works, they won't even hold hands before they get hitched. That gets me every time."

"It was the same for my wife and myself before we got married."

"Really? I didn't know that.'

Hakim has told him the same thing at least twice before but Schneider is, in one sense, a hotel guest so he does not correct him.

"Let us observe then," says Hakim. "I will top up your whisky in a minute."

The couple has sat down. The man is leaning forward across a low black table, his hands waving; he has removed his broad-rimmed black hat, exposing the skullcap beneath, also black.

The young woman sits opposite him, as is customary. Her arms, tightly folded, rest on a large handbag and she sits well back in the high-backed armchair. Her thin face is rigid yet watchful, a parody of paying attention.

"Not good, not good," says Schneider. "He looks the boastful type to me. Just talking about himself."

"She will take a phone call in ten minutes and leave.

I have seen her do this last week."

"Are you sure? I haven't seen her before."

"It was later in the evening. You were playing your medley from South Pacific. Your eyes were shut."

"Two old voyeurs." Schneider walks beside Hakim to the hotel bar, his back just a little more hunched than a week earlier.

The Housesitter
By Angela Lombardo

Such a big house for a small cat. Jen liked house sitting but this would be the first time the house included a cat.

She thought the house was like a museum but needed the money. She had worked in a claustrophobic office cubicle for ten years until the day she put a yellow sticky note on her dry erase board that said, *I Quit*.

The era was a mid-century hodgepodge. The living room had an orange shag rug and rectangular plastic furniture. A coffee table had a fondue tray on it.

Miss Laird, her new employer, looked like a model for an upscale resale shop. She was crisp, prim and wore an upswept hairstyle with curlicue sideburns and a mod, rectangular mini dress. She said she travelled constantly and would call with household instructions every morning at 7 o'clock sharp, pointing to a landline phone that had a rotary dial. Miss Laird left almost immediately wearing a pillbox hat and carrying vintage luggage. An envelope filled with cash to cover expenses for over a month sat on the coffee table.

Tabs, a gray cat with yellow eyes, followed as Jen inspected each room in the house. Most were empty except for shag carpeting of different colors. Digital clock radios were in every room and acknowledged the hour at different intervals of time. Her room was the same, except for a bed with a pink paisley comforter and nightstand.

One room was different – it looked like a TV area and vintage-style photos adorned the walls. All of them featured Miss Laird and another young woman with a blonde beehive hairstyle. In the photos Miss Laird was smiling and vibrant, in contrast to the frosty woman Jen had encountered. The pair wore stewardess uniforms from another era and they seemed to have traveled to many destinations. There was no remote for an ancient console TV with an antenna, so Jen turned it on manually and switched channels by turning a dial. All the programming seemed to be old reruns.

Jen took a short nap in her bedroom and was sound asleep when she heard the clock radio playing *Incense and Peppermints*. Tabs was alert and started meowing. A streetlight brightly illuminated the room, so Jen got up to close the window blind. She thought she saw Miss Laird peering up at her from the street shadows. Jen quickly pulled down the blind and ran back to the bed.

The numbers kept flipping on the clock radio and she woke up at 5.30 am. She went to the kitchen with Tabs and made coffee with a stove percolator. Fresh donuts were sitting on the counter next to an old piglet cookie jar. Miss Laird called at 7 o'clock sharp, rattled off a list of things for her to do and then tersely hung up.

After a day filled with mopping, scrubbing, washing and dusting, an aching Jen went to her bedroom for a short nap. Miss Laird was calling to her. She heard crying. She tiptoed to a nearby room, tripped over Tabs and fell to the floor . . .

Her cell phone was ringing when she woke up in bed. It was Madge from the temp agency who had placed her in the house. She seemed surprised Jen was still there. When Jen tried to tell her how odd Miss Laird was, Madge told her to keep up the good work and hung up.

She wasn't sure how she felt, if she was confused or afraid.

Tabs was always nearby, like a sentinel standing guard.

The landline was ringing continuously.

Jen finally stumbled to the phone. Someone was crying on the other end. The bright streetlight was glaring into the house again. She peered out of the front window and saw the woman with the beehive hairstyle staring at her from the sidewalk. Jen pulled the curtains shut and escaped to the bedroom with Tabs in tow.

Four o'clock in the morning, the old clock radio was playing *Good Morning Starshine* and there was wailing coming from that other room again. Jen decided it was time to go and gathered her purse and backpack. She went downstairs with Tabs and was about to leave when the ancient TV went on.

Miss Laird was in the TV box, demanding to know where she was going. Jen attempted to change the channel but Miss Laird was on all of them, chiding Jen for not cleaning out the bathroom properly.

Jen's resolve deserted her. She turned back up the stairs, Tabs now leading the way. She crept near the room with the crying and she timidly knocked on the door. The woman with the beehive hairstyle answered.

Jen felt like she was being sucked into the large room. Distant organ music played in the background. Empty rows of chairs seemed to point towards the wall. The smell of Tabu perfume was in the air. The woman with the beehive hairstyle took Jen's arm, escorting her as if they were in a solemn procession. Her touch was ice cold. She led Jen to Miss Laird, who was laying in a coffin. Jen felt sweaty with anxiety as Miss Laird opened her eyes and smiled, saying Jen didn't sweep under the kitchen table.

Grabbing her backpack, Jen nearly slid down the stairs and bolted to her old Chevy parked in the driveway. It was still dark outside, but she could see Miss Laird and Tabs watching from a lighted window as she sped away. *I'm a Believer* was playing on the car radio.

Jen never drove so fast or so far. At 10 in the morning she pulled up to a diner that advertised a full breakfast for a dollar forty-nine, complete with orange juice. Her cell phone rang with an *Incense and Peppermints* ringtone. It was Miss Laird, who briskly told her she was a lousy employee but she would give her good references.

Delete
By Laurel Lindstrom

Meredith March studies the wreck peering at her from the mirror and adds a touch more mascara to already overly mascara-ed eyes. She is always heavily made up, having never fully recovered from her Dusty Springfield circa '69 phase.

She's sitting at a mock rococo dressing table wrestling with curling tongs. The dressing table has three mirrors so there's no escape. The curling tong cable has folded back on itself in many places and refuses to straighten. Not in its nature. When Meredith tries to grab a lock of hair with the tongs, the tightly wound cable kinks, stiff and unyielding, knocking over bottles and assorted lipsticks. Stuff rolls to the edge of the dressing table. Meredith tries to stop things falling to the floor, but the tongs burn her cheek and tear her hair. Weak tears streak black under her eyes. Three sad faces remind her that she is tired and forgotten and life's pretense is overwhelming.

The dressing table vibrates. There's a message on her phone. "On way," it says. "Flight on time."

"Delete," she says. *Delete* and back to the primping which needs more care to be convincing. "Delete," says Meredith aloud at her three reflections, carefully unwinding her hair from the too-hot tongs. "Delete," she says again, dabbing cold cream on the red burn mark.

Delete. But then what?

What would she do instead, how would she persuade herself to do anything, go anywhere, see anyone if not for the stranger buckling up and peering out of the window at an airport monotony. He's her main topic of conversation, with her friends, with the children . . . But with them less often, they know how she feels about their dad. They understand.

She knows it isn't love with him, never was really. They don't know that. It's not lust any more, and they couldn't even go there. It faded in about year three. "When I was seven," she ponders, struggling into a loud floral print dress he bought her for Christmas.

Seven in dog years is 49. Too old to still be living in different countries. Too old to be waiting for him to get a London posting. Too long to be so old, so static, so floral, so tired. Too long for this same routine.

It wasn't so bad when the children were young. It

wasn't so bad when the money was a novelty, and the holidays too. New cars. Shopping with the girls. Inane gossip. Housey housey fixy upping. Following the lines. All of it too old. And now: *Delete*.

. . .

Downstairs, Meredith checks her black outfit in the hall mirror, florals now under the wheels of a dark revision. She searches for her car keys, checks the time, puts down food for the cat who's asleep on a sunny window ledge. He ignores her wistful stroke of his head.

Meredith takes frozen pastries out of the freezer. He likes those Danish cinnamon whirls.

She puts on her coat, picks up her bag and . . . *Delete*. Puts the bag down again and runs upstairs. Breathless, she finds her passport and retrieves her stash of 784 Euros in old holiday money. Waters a plant. Glances around the kitchen.

The journey to the airport is about as long as the flight from Madrid, give or take. There's no need to hurry. She ponders his appearance in arrivals. He'll be underdressed for the murky Manchester skies. He'll shiver as they leave the terminal. He'll say: "Ooh, so much colder than Madrid. I'll need to pick up a coat." He's coming back to his home town, but he likes to remind her of his difference, it will give them something to do, something to fill the space between them. Meredith hears the reruns of those filler conversations as she starts the car and switches off the radio. *Delete*. No distractions now.

. . .

The phone tracker app shows flight BA0461 casting its line across the sky. The M6 is slow as ever and Meredith March has time between stops to scan her phone, check flights, book parking in the short-term carpark. £20 should be enough. Sitting in the traffic, silent, another message on the phone. She texts back: "Yes, I know I booked parking." *Delete*.

It's Friday night. They can go and get him a coat tomorrow, hit the shopping mall masked and hand-sanitised and count the empty stores. He'll want a pub lunch. She'll explain that they can't. He'll tell her this commute will only be for another few months. And then he'll change the subject.

She turns on the radio: "A shooting in Tampa, Florida . . . " *Delete*. Tampa, Florida. We were there once. Flew in direct and spent two weeks arguing about alligators and sun cream with the children. Tampa. *Delete*.

Pulling into the short-term car park, watching the barrier bounce satisfyingly up, Meredith March smiles, parks and switches off the engine. She leaves the key on the rear passenger side tyre and turns away. She is early. There is time to kill. Kill or be killed. *Delete*.

. . .

When Mr March in his too-thin coat comes out of arrivals, his expensive four-wheeled carry-on in tow, Meredith is watching out of sight. She notes his handsome profile and the way his look slides across the people waiting, as he seeks her out. She's not quite ready to turn away.

She sees him frown, sees him tap at his phone and wonders why her phone isn't ringing. As Mr March stands legs astride his case, Meredith March heads quickly for Security before anything can happen to divert her. Amidst hoards of people she is reminded to social distance and to keep moving.

The bored security man in a purple turban is repeating his lines as he scans the queues, checking, always checking. "Laptops, tablets, shoes off, coats off, number four please, and madam to number two. Take off your jacket please."

Bang bang with the boxes, through the screener, then shoes on, coat on, tablet retrieved. Phone buzzing.

A host of duty free shops on the other side, a host of strangers, a host of new worlds. It's credit-card heaven in the Kurt Geiger shop with an excessively-made-up young woman, also channelling her inner Dusty. "Lovely make-up," Meredith can't help but say and the lovely young girl beams and pats her beehive. She hands over three bags with three new pairs of shoes and one with Meredith's discards. "I'll keep these on and you can keep the old ones," smiles Meredith, handing back the bag.

Next stop is an expensive Tumi expandable carry-on for the shoes and now the Hugo Boss Japanese stretch crepe jacket and matching trousers. The Hermés scarf. The Cartier watch. And the lingerie. And the many hundreds of pounds worth of Sisley make-up.

Another glamorous young woman is massaging her face and holding sample skin tones, head on one side quizzical, eyebrows tight, unfeasibly long fingernails flickering under artificial light. "You have wonderful skin, you know. Shall we try something a little different?"

"Yes, please," says Meredith. There's a message from him. "In arrivals." *Delete.*

She hands over the credit card and glimpses something a lot different in the mirror. She packs the new beauty regime in the new carry-on and heads for the cashpoint, teetering on her new heels. She withdraws maximum cash from all of his credit cards and has to sit down to stop from feeling dizzy. Picks up her phone again. "Waiting." *Delete.* "Are you held up?" *Delete.*

Meredith March steps away and checks her gate number, 46. Meredith March heads for the lounge. Sipping cava and picking at cheese she goes online and posts a picture on Facebook of her new suitcase and stilettoed feet with the message: "At airport still waiting for John."

She crafts a text message to their son: "When you get this, tell him the keys are on the tyre. Level 2 K32."

The phone is buzzing again but it's time for gate 46. Deep breath. Stand tall in those high heels. Tits and teeth. But that buzz. "Where are you?" *Delete*. As she wheels along in the high new shoes, behind her mask Meredith is gone. *Delete*.

George's Lockdown
By Kurt Whelan

A transparent globule is whitening rapidly in a whirlpool of hot water, clouding over its golden heart. George carefully scoops it out with a slotted culinary spoon, trying not to split it, to spoil it. It had taken him many hours and many failed attempts to achieve this level of poached-egg perfection. He's proud of this morning's success.

The toaster ejects a single charred slice with unnecessary violence. It drops hard onto the breadboard scattering a galaxy of darkness across the worktop. As he spreads an even layer of *I Can't Believe It's Not Butter* across the blackened bread, he listens attentively to the BBC.

The radio is in excellent condition but it's over 25 years old and only receives AM/FM signals. At the back of his mind is the nagging thought that this will be useful when the digital network is switched off. He's not sure why he thinks this but he feels it is inevitable, pushing him deeper into isolation. He has a supply of batteries – enough, he thinks, to keep him tuned in to the rest of the world for around six months during the expected power outages.

Today's news tells of yet more cancellations, lockdowns, border closures and a growing list of nation states in siege mode. There are no more mass gatherings. No sport, theatre, concerts, baptisms, weddings. There are funerals. There have to be funerals. They've closed the schools and universities. The airports, train stations, and ferry terminals; no one is going anywhere. Echoing the vision of the future Orwell had imagined, the message is everywhere: STAY INDOORS! DO NOT TRAVEL! Hospitals resemble military encampments. Our empty streets are patrolled by soldiers dressed in bio-hazard suits. There's a rumour – they have orders to shoot on sight those who break curfew. *Is there a curfew?* He turns off the radio.

George has not been out of his house for weeks. He recalls the posters he saw on his last trip to the city; images of people in surgical masks. KEEP YOUR DISTANCE! NO TOUCHING! It's been almost a month since the government information films were released: *Kiss Your Grandmother To Death* along with *Your Child: A Viral Timebomb!* and *Don't Be A Selfish Superspreader*. All acts of affection – kissing, hand-holding, engaging in sexual congress – are vigorously discouraged.

Six feet, around two metres he thinks, recalling those happy times in Italy and France. The government are calling it Social Distancing. Stand apart! Move away! DO NOT MAKE CONTACT! DO NOT TOUCH!

It is good that they care for our welfare, he thinks. *We need to be told what to do. We are irresponsible fools, sad idiots with immortality complexes.*

Remain Indoors! Keep your windows closed and doors locked! Keep calm! Remember, the soldiers are there for your protection. Do not panic! DO NOT PANIC! He doesn't panic. He watches the television as he eats his egg on toast.

The Prime Minister has a special announcement for the nation – a simultaneous broadcast across all major networks. He's barely recognisable, dressed head to foot in white decontamination coveralls. The elasticated hood is tight around his fleshy reddening face, his famous blond locks tucked out of sight. Where now that japester, the nation's fun-loving jolly buffoon? He raises his visor, a full-face covering of transparent plexiglass. There's a hiss as the respirator uncouples from the oxygen supply. His eyes dart nervously about, then settle on the bank of remotely-controlled cameras. They are arranged behind a transparent perspex wall, their operators safely in isolation pods, scattered across the gardens of Parliament Square. The statue of Winston Churchill looks down on them, his scowl preserved forever in bronze. You can almost hear the angry warrior spitting contempt.

The PM stands alone. His small entourage of ministers, all similarly attired, stand well back. Their identity is unclear, the lanyards hanging beneath their helmeted heads are illegible through the disinfecting mist. Unseen by the cameras, sharpshooters are keeping watch on rooftops, in doorways and behind trees – but there is no target; no law-breaking multitude, no riotous rabble, no unhappy conflagration. Like George, the great unwashed are all at home watching their TVs, laptops, tablets, smartphones. They're waiting for their leader to speak to them, to reassure them, to tell them what to do. They're waiting impatiently for what will probably be the most important speech they will ever hear in their sadly-shortened lives.

The PM steps closer to the array of microphones. He tries to smile through his nervousness. As if a voice in his earpiece was shrieking, "No! Do not smile! Do NOT smile!" – his inappropriate grin dissolves in an instant. His HazMat suit crackles as he moves. He coughs. A nervous cough. A dry cough. A collective flinch sweeps through Parliament Gardens. The out-of-focus ministers react skittishly like frightened deer. They step further back into the safe zone.

"Sorry, er … Just clearing my throat. I'm, er… you know. I'm okay now, I'm over that." So begins the PM's historic announcement. He continues, "People of Britain . . . " George listens without really hearing. "Throughout the history of our great nation . . . " A seemingly endless stream of platitudes follows. "We have withstood greater threats . . . " His words empty, anachronistic, patronising. "Together we will overcome . . ."

The PM drones on for almost ten more minutes before reaching the inevitable patriotic climax. The script, prepared in haste by the best available writers, ends with words which strike George as condescending and trite, "Above all, remember you are British. Stay calm. Remain indoors! Though six feet apart, we're all in this together!"

He steps away from the microphone and lowers his visor. His face disappears from the condensation gathering inside the plastic shell. A couple of decon-suited attendants briefly assist him with his respirator before scurrying back through a cloud of atomised disinfectant to the safety zone. Safe distances are maintained. The PM stops briefly, looks back at the cameras and attempts a reassuring but unchoreographed wave of a gloved hand.

He climbs alone into the back of the armoured personnel carrier. A BBC director, with faultless patriotic timing, cuts to a remote-controlled camera aimed at the statue of Churchill. A lone herring gull is perched on the great man's bald head. The bird stands proud, its beautiful plumage barely ruffled by the afternoon breeze. It opens its bright yellow bill and lets out a harsh, repetitive, mocking laugh. It surveys the gardens with cold, pale eyes. There's nothing, not a scrap. Everything edible long-since eaten. It unfurls its great wings, shamelessly disgorging the contents of its avian cloaca just before taking to the air. A speckled bead of liquid guano runs down the old man's bronze head leaving a white streak from his brow-ridge to his corpulent cheek. It comes to rest on the broad lapel, like a medal on the puffed-up chest.

George switches off the television and sits back in his chair. Solitude. How long has it been now? He wonders what all the fuss is about; the panic over isolation and quarantine. *That's just life! Has it ever been any other way?* After a few moments staring at a blank screen, he gets up from the chair. He walks into the kitchen. The PM's vacuous words are already fading from his mind.

He opens the utility room door and scans the contents. Once the panic had begun, the hoarding of non-perishables became the new national pastime. Toilet rolls and paracetamol; the new banknotes, the new coinage. Tinned sardines, corned beef, canned soup, flour and dried pasta; suddenly the latest must-have items of desire.

George had other ideas about life's bare necessities.

On three walls, from floor to ceiling, are his hastily-constructed storage racks. Hardly works of woodcraft, more utilitarian. Their beauty is their purpose and their purpose is their contents. Each shelf holds a row of green bottles, all lying in peaceful repose, foil-covered corks and screw-tops (he's no purist) the only visible identifying marker. Some of the best his local outlets had on offer, classic favourites; Shiraz from Australia, Chilean Merlot, South African Pinotage, Spanish Rioja.

Enough to last until autumn, he thinks, smiling smugly. He pulls out an old familiar friend and examines the gold, black and red label, the little starling with the top hat and bow-tie; a Pfalz unfiltered 2016. A German Black Star from his local Aldi. The blood-red contents dark as midnight through the bottle-green glass. Caressing the gentle curves with a non-too-subtle eroticism, George lets a flood of memories course through his mind. 2016, before the madness. 2016, when there was still hope. 2016, when he believed there was still everything to live for. He pulls the cork and reaches for a glass.

The Sense of You
By Richard Copestake

The dim glow of the clock behind me outlines the soft cotton contour of your shoulder, a horizon beyond which all is dark and still. The almost imperceptible rise and fall of your breathing is the only movement in this warm, quiet moment where nothing exists but the heat of your presence.

Your warmth gently bathes my face as we lie spooned together, conjoined all the way down. I wonder how many hours we've spent like this. How many more there will be?

That first night two generations ago was nothing like this. Sweaty, nervous and juvenile. Do you want the left side of the bed or the right? Switching over and over through the night. Hot accidental touches quickly pulled away – sorry! No, it was my fault – sorry! The bedding increasingly tangled around our naked bodies as we struggled to settle, moist and dulled for a while from earlier fumblings and quickly-spent passion. Rising again from time to time in the humid midsummer darkness until by dawn we were more exhausted than when we'd stumbled upstairs long hours earlier.

Whole nights spent together before we married were rare and intoxicating. Youthful excitement in each other mixed with the thrill of breaking the rules. Your dorm when your roommate was away, a knowing older cousin's spare room for a weekend, a cheap bed and breakfast on the coast when we were both supposed to be somewhere else. We learned about each other through intimate hours in the dark; where to touch, how to kiss, when to yield.

And in those unexpected or opportune moments; walking hand in hand through the forest and realising we were completely alone, by the fire's glow on a familiar old sofa when parents were out, or in the dubious privacy of my old Vauxhall in a moonlit layby.

Three beautiful babies came along in their own good time, adding curves to your once-skinny body and gently swelling your breasts to an exquisite fullness. You don't stir as I lightly caress the warm cushion of your hip, now comfortably padded over the bony contours where this hand has rested so often, the very cradle of the family we created together.

It took thirty years from the firstborn cry to the last one leaving home.

Quite suddenly they were gone and unexpectedly, we began to discover each other all over again. Hello, my old friend, do you remember me?

We started taking walks along the beach and sitting together in companionable silence, doing not much at all. One day we took a trip to France on the spur of the moment and savoured being able to choose a restaurant without having to consider whether the menu would suit everyone. We travelled light with little more than a change of underwear and a spongebag.

We found ourselves holding hands a lot and after a little too much wine we kissed with a passion long forgotten in the shadow of something monumentally French. You laughed a little too much as I replayed a lifetime of trivia, prompted by some landmark or other. We took selfies and posted silly pictures on Facebook like our kids do.

We discovered a new intimacy. Affectionate and undemanding, lying in each other's arms with no use for the fervour of our youth, hardly needing more than close contact in the night. And through the daylight hours too. It was a different kind of honeymoon that didn't end with the jolt of wheels landing on tarmac. It won't end until we do.

The faint halo of your hair is a tangle of curls, natural and always lovely to me, hated and brushed vigorously straight each day by you. I once asked why brushing it was the first thing you did when you got out of bed, but I don't remember your answer. You still do it and I still wish you wouldn't. But it doesn't matter.

The hair at the nape of your neck lightly brushes my forehead as you stir a little. Hints of shampoo and toothpaste mingle with remnants of the perfume you have worn all our married life and with those elemental essences that define you alone. This is the breath I inhale from your pillow when you leave the bed in the morning.

I have breathed you on three continents, in bustling cities and quiet countryside, in hotels, narrowboats and everywhere that we have called home. For sweet moments after every affectionate embrace, a scented echo of your presence remains in my nose and on my lips.

I cannot resist touching my lips to those fine downy hairs again, drawing in the fragrance of your presence. I have covered every inch of this body with gentle kisses and at times I have consumed it with fierce passion. Such delicate skin, so sensitive and responsive in our lovemaking. I'm tempted to brush your ear with a kiss – you always liked that – and I long for you to turn over and offer again those soft tender lips to mine, but I dare not bring you from that restful place you have found tonight.

I listen to the rhythm of your breathing, slowly in . . . and . . . out . . . . You don't talk in your sleep like you used to. Your head was once filled with lessons to prepare and marking to finish. Nights were an unwelcome interruption to all that needed to be done and your brain punished you with strange dream journeys. You would shout incomprehensible nonsense and startle us both into clammy wakefulness that would banish all prospect of sleep for hours to come.

Sometimes you still give a little whimper or add voice to an exhaled breath, but it seldom wakes you now. I lie awake for hours beside you, sleep no longer a priority for me in these quieter days when every moment with you is so precious. Occasionally you wake yourself with a snort and giggle yourself back to sleep at the ridiculousness of it, unaware that in the dark I am grinning too.

I tune my own breathing to yours, in . . . and . . . out . . . I am at one with you, our pulses beat as one, as our thoughts and ideas have done so often down the years and more than ever these days. You read my mind about when it's time to put the kettle on, I know exactly when to speak and when to just silently hold you.

The first hint of dawn is beginning to outline the curtained window beyond you. I silently pray that many more dawns will come. A blackbird pierces the silence outside, declaring his virility to his mate.

I nuzzle my face into the back of your neck and breathe, "I love you."

"I love you too," you whisper back.

Room 304
By Ed Walsh

It was way back, April 1968, and I had been seeing Miriam Grady for two years. She was a perfume buyer for Goldsmiths and came into the city occasionally from Tunica, to the south, where she lived with her husband and her kid. I was at Germantown, to the east, with my wife and my two kids.

Occasionally we stayed somewhere in the city; but mainly we got together in one of the small towns like Henderson or Palestine, somewhere we just picked out on the map. We went to different places each time, we somehow thought that that would reduce the risk of exposure. I'm not sure where we got that idea from, and thinking back I'm not sure there was any sense to it.

It had started when I had a few days' work in Lewisburg – I'm a surveyor for the Water Authority and I spend some periods on the road. I was down there by myself and having my evening meal in one of the restaurants just off the town square. Miriam Grady too was there for one night with her work and was seated at the next table, also alone. We got talking and, as the saying goes, one thing led to another. I won't go into detail but she excited me like I had never before been excited, and I say that as someone who has a great love for his wife.

So that was the problem, one of them anyway. We continued meeting but the guilt did not go away. I knew that with one wrong move, the whole thing could blow up. For some men I know, some colleagues, such a thing is of no more consequence to them than switching on the television. Married men I'm talking about, some with kids, who have one woman after another and barely make a secret of it. One I know has a kid with another woman, although his wife doesn't know about it. How do people do that, lead the two lives? Me, I didn't have the stomach.

So, this time I was going to tell Miriam how great she was, but that I could only lead the one life at a time – and that life had to be with my wife and kids in Germantown.

I told my wife that I had to go across to Clarksville one night, but instead booked a room for me and Miriam to stay at the Lorraine Motel on Mulberry Street. The routine was the same most places we stayed. We would both get there around 3, do what we did, then get room service, just to avoid any unnecessary risk, and spend the night together. She would ring me at my office when it was okay to meet again.

This time though, there was trouble in the city and a curfew. The sanitation workers were on strike and were marching most days. They wanted better pay and conditions and who could blame them; in my job I had seen what they did close up and most of it wasn't pleasant – certainly most whites didn't want to do it. But Loeb, who was the mayor then, wasn't having any of it. I supported the workers and would always put money into their buckets.

Anyway, because of the marches the traffic was rerouted. King had come down to support them and I heard his speech on the car radio, the one where he talked about the promised land. Whatever side of the line you were on, he was a good speaker, and he stood up for his people. Some – the people who didn't like him – made comments about his private life but, even if I had wanted to, I was in no position to talk.

I saw the men who were striking. I drove slowly past them and they weren't causing any trouble. Some of them wore placards saying I AM A MAN. I wondered, could I wear a placard like that and feel it was right, doing what I had been doing. What kind of a man was I? I wasn't sure I'd like the answer to that. But at least I was about to do the right thing. It seemed like a good time to end it too.

We were going out to the coast at the weekend for two weeks. The year before, I couldn't relax; just watching my kids on the beach and thinking of Miriam Grady and what I was doing with her cut me up too much. This time I wanted my mind free.

I was given a key for 304. Miriam too was re-routed and got there about an hour later. I was nervous and wanted to get it done and over with. I told her straightaway, that it was great to see her but that we had to talk. It wouldn't have seemed fair waiting until afterwards. I told her how I thought the world of her and I hoped she knew that but that I couldn't carry on the way I was. And she cried, not because she was upset at the ending of the thing, but because she had wanted to say the same thing and was wondering how to do it without hurting me. That set me off and we both cried, and we held each other, and we decided not to stay the night. So, we wished each other a great life and checked out again at 5.

I rang my wife from the lobby. I told her that I got the Clarksville work done early. The streets were quieter as I drove east out of the city. Some of the placards had been discarded and were lying on the sidewalk.

That evening, Cronkite came on while we were eating. He said King had been shot an hour earlier – *Shot to death*, was the phrase he used. It turned out he was staying at that same motel – the Lorraine. Not only that, but he was staying in the next room – 306. He had stepped out onto the balcony and someone had shot him – Cronkite said the bullet exploded in his face. They didn't know who had fired the shot.

So, while Miriam and I were saying our final goodbyes, Mr King – on the other side of the wall, if he was in there – was an hour or so away from being shot. If we had stayed longer we would have heard the shots and been close up to what I was watching on the screen now. I could see room 304 behind the reporter's head. And the President came on and spoke about it. It was something I wanted to speak about too, about that strange coincidence, about my proximity to such an event and to such a man, but there was no one I could tell. There was only my wife there, shaking her head at the horror on our screen and asking what the world was coming to.

That was a good while back, but I still think about it. I'm still out in Germantown, but I drive along Mulberry Street occasionally. They turned the motel into a museum for him. And whenever I drive past there I think of Miriam and wonder how she is, and how she might be doing. I can still make out the room where we said our goodbyes, and the balcony where King was shot.

The Monkey Puzzle Tree
By Gwenda Major

In the fading light of the graveyard the burning end of the spliff was the only bright point in the gloom.

"Hand it over, mate. My turn." Rob plucked the roll-up from his friend's fingers and took a deep drag. He giggled. "What did you tell your mam?"

"Same as usual. Youth club – playing ping pong."

"Ping pong? Ping pong? Whatyouonabout?"

"Ping pong. Table – you know – tennis." Tommo sounded unsure now. "What about you anyway?"

"What about me?"

"What did you tell your mam?"

"Nothing. She didn't ask. Never does."

"Sweet."

"Yeah."

From the main road the shriek of a siren swelled and subsided. Around them loomed the grotesque silhouettes of the huge pine trees.

"Look at that," Rob said, his words coming out slurred.

"What?"

"That. That tree over there." Rob sat up on the bench where he'd been sprawling and tried to focus his eyes properly. Gravestones stuck up from the earth like black teeth all around them. It was quiet. The perfect place to smoke a spliff – which they did most Friday nights. No-one seemed to notice. And they weren't hurting anybody.

"That's a monkey puzzle," Tommo announced authoritatively after a lengthy pause.

"You what?"

"A monkey puzzle. It's a tree."

"I know it's a tree. But it's a fucking weird tree."

"Yeah well they are weird – monkey puzzle trees. Very weird."

The two sat in silence for a while, peacefully passing the spliff from hand to hand. Apart from the distant rumble of traffic there was no sound. Rob closed his eyes, drifted off for a few minutes.

"My mam used to scare me with it," Tommo said eventually.

Rob roused himself and peered at his friend's face. "How d'ya mean?"

"When we walked home through the graveyard – she'd tell me to keep quiet when we got near the monkey puzzle, else I'd grow a monkey tail."

"She never?"

"She did. And I believed her."

"Oi, Tommo – don't look now but there's something growing out of your arse." Rob had staggered to his feet and was dancing around the bench making monkey noises, arms swinging from side to side. Then he tripped over his own feet and fell to the ground.

"Shit!"

"Serves you right. Moron."

"Just a bit of fun, mate," Rob muttered, rubbing his leg as he levered himself up.

"Anyway, my gran said that wasn't right," Tommo continued.

"See – just your mam being daft."

"No – my gran said you have to keep quiet because the Devil lives up the monkey puzzle and if he hears you, he'll come down and get you."

"She said that?"

"Swear to God."

"And you believed her?"

"Nah. She was probably pissed at the time. She liked a drink – or two or three, my gran."

"I'm getting cold," Rob said suddenly. "Come on."

"Where're we going?"

"Come on," Rob repeated, following the narrow path

between the gravestones to the brow of the hill which was dominated by the silhouette of the huge monkey puzzle tree. The sun was setting now, lending an apricot glow to the sky. Like a vast spiky umbrella, the tree's branches seemed to lean down to stroke the scatter of gravestones at its base. Each branch ended in a gentle curve just like the end of a monkey's tail. Rob reached the tree first and flung his arms around the vast gnarled trunk.

"Here, Tommo – hold hands."

"I thought you'd never ask."

"Ha ha. Here – reach round." The two friends joined hands around the tree, their faces pressed into the trunk, breathing noisily.

"I dare you to climb it," Tommo said after they let go. "Like a monkey."

"You're having a laugh. There's no branches at the bottom. Look."

They both gazed up at the full height of the tree.

"It's fucking enormous. It must be 20 metres."

"More like 30 – or 40."

"Whatever – it's big." Tommo reached out and grasped one of the branches. "Ow! That hurt."

"Course it fucking hurt. It's spiky. Anyone could see that."

"Well thanks for the warning, mate." Tommo was getting bored.

Rob gazed upwards to where the mass of branches formed a whorl against the sky. Tipping his head back made him feel dizzy and he shut his eyes.

When he opened them again he stumbled and fell, his knees hitting one of the swollen knuckles at the base of the monkey puzzle.

Under the canopy of the tree the quiet had taken on an intensity that made Rob's ears buzz. All the colour had leached from the sky. He was surrounded by the dark humps of the gravestones and he felt cold. A deep cold that seemed to chill his bones.

"Tommo?" he said, peering around in the darkness. No answer.

"Tommo? Come on, mate. Stop farting about. I don't like it here. I'm going home." Still no answer. If Tommo was trying to scare him it was working. Rob managed to get himself on to both knees and carefully turned his head from side to side. All he could make out were the shadowy slabs of the gravestones.

"Tommo. Please. Where are you? Come on, mate." But this time he didn't really expect a reply.

Rob felt a vibration through his left hand, still touching the trunk of the tree. The curved arms of the monkey puzzle were trembling slightly, as if someone was slowly climbing down the tree. Frozen in terror, he waited.

Scarlet Lipstick
By Angela Aries

After all this time, she could still taste his blood.

Of course, she had lied to the policewoman. She had stood there with her mother in the dark hallway, a gangling 13-year-old, twining her left leg awkwardly behind her right ankle, and answering the inevitable questions.

Did she always go out at the same time? Had she taken the dog a different way? Had anything like that ever happened before?

Well, yes, she did go out at about the same time, when she got back from school. Sometimes she changed, after having a cup of tea. Then she took the dog round the block, sometimes following the crescent round to the right, by the boys' school playing field, sometimes in the opposite direction. No, nothing like this had ever happened before. Nobody following her anyway.

What she dared not, or could not articulate, and what

the policewoman did not need to know, was the reason why she had changed her clothes. She had left the school uniform on but removed the white socks and brown strapped sandals and had put on a suspender belt and stockings, which wrinkled annoyingly round her ankles. Then she had slipped on her beige casuals, a birthday present from her aunt, wound a flowery scarf round her neck and applied a thick coat of scarlet to her lips. It was a cool day, so she grabbed her navy mac and belted it tight at the waist.

She had turned left this time, hoping she might spot good-looking Peter walking his spaniel, but had gone a bit further on than usual. Well, she told the woman, she had taken the path over the heathland which led past the ruined fort. And yes, it was out of sight of the main road.

The questions that followed had been tricky. When did she first notice the man? Could she describe him? What happened next? Then, cautiously, what did he do? Did he hurt her? She supposed she first saw him along the path to the fort. He was tall, curly-haired, and a bit scruffy looking. His age? No idea. When she thought he was following her, she walked more quickly. He did the same. Afraid, she started running across the grass. She fell, tripping over the enormous tufts of grass. She screamed. The dog stood beside her, bewildered. The man knelt down and put his hands over her mouth. She bit him, so he let go. He got up and ran off. No, he did not hurt her. Yes, she was sure. No, nothing else.

The truth was, she had wanted him to follow her at first. But when she realised how rough he looked, how unkempt and unshaven, she had panicked. She ran, so did he, tracking her down as she fled. When she stumbled and fell, he leapt on top of her. She felt his hot breath on the back of her neck. He had clapped both hands round her mouth to try and stop her screaming and she bit as hard as she could. He roared with pain, cursed, and released his hold. Getting off her quickly, he shot off down the path towards the town. She got up and ran home.

Had he done anything else, enquired the policewoman. Her mother watched anxiously on. No, she said. The officer persisted, and she resolutely repeated the version she had already given. In truth, she was surprised the man had not tried to force her over on her back. But then, she really was not at all sure how people had sex. Was it facing one another? She thought so. Had he meant to attack her? Had she encouraged him? Was it her fault? Was it the scarlet lipstick perhaps? She blushed. Now her armpits were all sweaty, and her stomach began to gripe.

She hopped uneasily from one foot to the other. Faced with this stranger in uniform, she clenched her fists, averted her reddening cheeks, and stared at the floor. She refused to say any more. The policewoman shut her notebook, seemingly dissatisfied. "Well, if that really is everything, I'll be off." Then, turning to her mother she added, "We will be in touch of course, if we catch the man."

She moistened her thin lips. Yes, it must have been more than 60 years ago, but the iron taste still lingered in her mouth.

The Life of Riley
By Chris Milner

It was another sunny day in paradise. Outside, the breeze was gently waving the trees at me. I watched bees bob across the rhododendrons just under the window. Up above, clouds oozed across the azure canvas, performing their merry dance before gently dissipating.

"Here you go, Riley," says the girl, putting a cup of coffee on the table beside me. "Just how you like it. Are you enjoying your Saturday sunshine?"

And that's when he turns up, large as life and twice as ugly.

"Hello, son," I say, happy to get a visitor. "You here for the coffee?"

"I've come to see you, uncle," he says, and smirks, like he's got a little secret he's keeping to himself.

"Do I know you, son?" I say. "My memory's not so good now, see."

"It's me, uncle. Harry. You remember me. I come every day, almost."

Anyway, that's what *he* says, but how do I know?

"Well, it's nice to get a visitor, son. Pull up a bench and sit yourself down here. But that girl's giving out drinks, so go and see if she's got any biscuits before you do. I like a biscuit."

When he comes back, he tells me he's brought some photos for me.

"Oh, yes," I say. "Nothing incriminating, I hope. Not trying blackmail, are you son? You don't look like a blackmailer. Too pale. Too tall. Not that I'm saying I know what a blackmailer looks like, am I?"

"No, no," says the lad and smirks again. "I thought you might like to see these pictures. See if you can remember anyone."

"Okay, son. Sounds good to me. Fire away."

He pulls an envelope from his jacket pocket, slips a photo out and passes it to me with an expectant face, like he's showing me a winning race ticket. It's a picture of a woman in a long white dress, leaning against a wooden post.

"Full throttle poser, I'd say," I tell him. "Nice legs."

"Do you recognise her?" he asks, watching me closely with a 'big moment' look crunching up his eyes.

"Should I?"

"It's Elsie," he says. "On the pier at Branksome. Must

have been taken soon after you were married."

I'm not sure what to say to that. The woman in the picture looks back happily as I study her face, trying hard to remember her, to pull something out.

"Nice," I tell the lad. "Pity I didn't meet her before I got hitched."

He smiles, in that brave but crestfallen way. A man who's not going to admit how much he's just lost on the Derby.

"Let's try this one."

He slips another of the pictures out from his collection. This one's in colour. There's a guy with a yellow vest over his jacket, sporting a peaked captain's hat. He's spread out over a deckchair with a bottle of pop in his hand, like he's got nothing to do all day. It's sunny enough to burn the bank and the guy, who's got himself quite the tan, looks as happy as Larry.

"I wouldn't mind his job," I say, because the boy is expecting me to say something.

I can see this is disappointing him again and he goes all moody quiet for a bit. But then his face takes a sudden turn.

"I've had a great idea," he announces, now all smiles. "Have you finished that coffee, uncle?"

"Well, I wouldn't mind another biscuit," I say.

"Let's have a little outing, shall we. Just us. No need to worry the staff. We'll just pop out. Be back in time for lunch." And he's up and releasing the brakes on my chair and pushing me out of the room before I can say Jiminy Cricket.

Outside the room, there's a corridor. I can see the front door on my right, and one of the girls ushering someone in, but the lad is steering me the other way. We pass a series of doors, go down a ramp, past the clatter from some kitchens and out into the air. It's bright out there and I tell him, "Hold up, son. Where are we going? You kidnapping me? You won't get much, you know. No-one's going to pay the ransom. I've left strict instructions about that."

"Don't worry, uncle," he says. "We're going to have some fun."

"Good clean fun, I hope, son. I'm not up to much of the other kind, anymore."

But then he stops next to a grubby little red car, opens the door, and helps me up.

"In you go, uncle. You're going to enjoy this."

I can tell he's breaking the law. He's hurrying everything, snatching guilty looks back at the house. As soon as I'm in, he collapses the chair, loads it into the boot, scurries round to the driver's side, climbs in and starts up. The wheels kick up the gravel as we scoot out of the gate.

. . .

As we run down the road, he settles to a steadier pace.

"Okay, uncle?" he asks, a little breathlessly. "Must be a while since you were last on an outing."

"Must be," I say.

The houses give way to open fields and little woodlands, dressing the gently curving hills that work away from the road. You can't see anything move from inside a car. The trees are frozen as you dodge past. You scoot past clouds and birds in flight, like they were painted on the sky.

"Does that look familiar?" he asks, as the ruin of Corfe Castle looms up on our right.

"Of 'corfe' it does," I say, and give him a grin and I think I've made his day.

"Know where we're going?" he asks.

"Not a clue," I admit. "But it's good to be out. Can we find a toilet, soon?"

We continue past the fields and woodlands for a bit, before turning down a narrow track. *Studland*, says the sign and, soon after that, we pull up in a parking area. A bloke with a yellow vest over his jacket comes over, pushes his peaked cap back from his damp forehead and says to the lad, "Three quid for the day, mate."

The boy looks expectantly at me again. I've no idea why.

"You're on your own, son," I tell him. "I haven't any cash."

I can tell he's frustrated again, but he parks the car, gets the chair out and helps me into it. "Let's take a look around, shall we. See if you remember anything."

It's downhill from here, the track weaving to and fro between heavily laden hedgerows. There's the chattering of blackbirds and the jabber of nesting swallows all around us. Is that the sort of thing he wants me to remember? There's a strong smell of the sea, too. I remember that. Should I tell him?

When we get to the end of the lane, the path runs over gravel alongside the large and rolling dunes. From the other side of the dunes, I can hear the sea playing with the beach, falling and retreating, falling and retreating.

There's a large car that's come down the road and been abandoned between the dunes on our left. As we approach it, a couple walk off the beach and cross the path in front of us, making their way towards it. Neither of them is wearing a stitch, and neither of them is still in their prime, and it's obvious their equipment just isn't in tip-top condition anymore.

"Tsch!" I say. "Shouldn't have parked there."

"This place ringing any bells for you, uncle?" the lad asks me.

"Not really, son, sorry," I say. "But we'd better find that toilet soon or I'm going to make a mess on the way back."

. . .

It was another sunny day in paradise. Outside, the breeze was gently waving the trees at me. I watched bees bob across the rhododendrons just under the window. Up above, clouds oozed across the azure canvas, performing their merry dance before gently dissipating.

"Here you go, Riley," says the girl, putting a cup of coffee on the table beside me. "Just how you like it. Another lovely day, isn't it?"

And that's when he turns up, large as life and twice as ugly.

"Hello, son," I say, happy to get a visitor. "You here for the coffee?"

Bubbles
By Michael Coutts

". . . and if you leave the A688 at Staindrop the B6274 will take you to the A66 and you're on the A1 at Scotch Corner before you know it."

"No. *No!* It's quicker if you leave the motorway at junction 11 and take the slip road out to . . . "

June held her brimming champagne glass against her nose and watched the conversation over the fluid surface while tiny bursts prickled her eyes. One of the speakers was heavy low down like a goose, the other had beaky lips. June scarcely knew a soul. She looked round for rescue and it came in the form of a man of about 40, her age, all bony in his suit and with a leaning forward sort of tallness. He stood too close; she'd get a stiff neck.

"What d'you drive?" he asked.

"Oh, no. I keep rabbits." She gave a little laugh.

"Rab . . . ?" He waited a smile's length but his mouth

remained straight. "What do you drive?"

She took a prolonged sip to gain time and her glass was immediately refilled. The blue eyes looking down at her were serious, demanding attention.

"Well I don't, you see. Not if I can help it."

"How d'you get about?"

"Oh, I don't."

His head came down further in a studying way and she wondered if he was a skin specialist. The nail of the thumb he placed against his chin was a perfectly manicured crescent.

"You don't go out?"

"No, I stay in. My rabbits."

"Look, you've only got to drive over to the B698 and you can be on the way to Bradford in 20 minutes. Or you can turn off earlier and explore one of those little unmetalled roads in the hills."

She took another swig from her magical self-filling glass. Bubbles fumed in her brain. She stood on tiptoe to get even closer to him – they were almost kissing – and began to sing quietly:

"The A road is connected to the . . . B road,

And the B road is connected to the . . . C road,

And the C road is connected to the . . . unmetalled road.

Hear the word of the Lord."

His pupils seemed to be receding but they were merely

contracting in shock. She tilted her head to the flat white ceiling and wished for cherubs. Instead, two men arrived from opposite directions, simultaneously smiling at her and glaring at each other for spoiling what each had planned to do to her.

"What do you . . . "

"How did you . . . " Mr North was convex with bulgy eyes (blue, again); Mr South was concave with eyes hidden in crevices. Both had red faces. Mr South with an orange tinge.

I'm a marigold, she thought. She opened her eyes wide as a marigold at Mr South but the crevices remained, even closed a little, no telling the colour of his eyes; she just hoped they were blue. He toasted an imaginary friend and escaped.

Mr North still liked her as she was, so she preened a little to reward him with a glimpse of silicone valley. His mouth was dropping open, perhaps shaping up for words, so she tried to beat him to it.

"What do you drive?" they both said.

He bulged more now, with excitement.

"A JX3-47. Sixteen valves, nought to a hundred-and-ten in eleven seconds!"

"*What* a long way," she said, and smoothed his lapels, which were getting quite ruffled. She handed him her glass, stood straight as a soldier. Right . . . turn! She clasped her hands under her chin and made three bunny hops away from him and three back.

"Cherubs," she said, and was about to pinch his cheeks when her first couple, who were honking most dreadfully, distracted her. They had arrived in France but by different, terribly contentious routes; she had not known motoring was so fraught.

"You're joking. I've done Edinburgh to Dover in seven hours without even trying."

"You bloody haven't, not that route, you know what it's like around Stevenage!"

Their beaks swung to her for support. She sang more loudly: "The A road is connected to the . . . B road."

People were looking now; it was nice; she'd never been a turner of heads. Silence was spreading out through the party. She trotted up and down, her heels making a ruinous clacking on the parquet.

"The B road is connected to the . . ." she tapped her leg, "thigh road."

"The thigh road is connected to the . . ." she tapped again, "knee road."

She thrust her leg up like a dancer to reach her ankle.

"The knee road is connected to the . . . ankle road." She was taking short cuts, they wouldn't like it. She began to work her way up her leg and was approaching Junction 11 when her host appeared beside her, solicitous, soaked in embarrassment.

"Perhaps . . ." he took her elbow.

She shot her arms above her head:

"Altogether now! The head road is connected to the . . . neck road."

Two of the younger ones, just youths really, joyfully took her up on it:

"And the neck road is connected to the . . . shoulder road."

There were ripples now, increasing, a tide, a great swell, very soon the whole room was thumping and roaring. So this was what power felt like.

"The breast road," she banged them both, "is connected to the . . . back road."

She began to rotate and found herself inches from the skin man. He was, she saw, frightened, stuck, pickled in aspic. She took his hands and clapped them together.

"The hand roads are connected to the . . . wrist roads."

He was coming out of shock, his eyes zooming towards her as his pupils dilated. He began gesticulating like a scarecrow in a gale.

She tried turning her head to look in every corner but there was no need, the room was rotating about her, the floor thundering. No one languished, all were with her, even the couple last seen in France were bopping and slapping their knees and Mr South's crevices were open.

Blue, she'd known it! A hat trick! She kissed her hands and flung them to the crowd.

"Hear the word of the Lord!"

A Walk in the Park
By Brian McDonald

Every day the same routine. Down the slope. Over the ornamental bridge. Along the avenue. Up the hill. Around the ponds. Back down to the bridge. At first, she had run it. Jogging gear on, *Caribou* pounding through headphones. Then she walked, taking time to notice what was happening around her.

Over the weeks she had seen the trees put on blossom and leaf. Witnessed mating displays. Now goslings skitter across the lake. Today it had seemed she was going to be late. A pointless Zoom conference had gone on and on, everyone pretending that they were getting things done. In fact, the timing proved perfect. The sun had just left but there was still enough light to get round. Best of all she almost had the route to herself. Kids were back at home with their parents. The loud gangs of teenagers, carrier bags clanking with beer and nitrous oxide cylinders, drawing suspicious glances from plastic plods and the real police who are suddenly taking an interest in the park. All gone.

Even the hordes of dog walkers have thinned out. The local canines will be fit as a fiddle by the time this pandemic is over, if it ever is. So, no need to keep swerving sideways to maintain the correct social distance. Or wait with exaggerated patience at a bottleneck for some oblivious, dozy-arse to move on. She can just stride out, free and alone. That is, until she sees the body.

He is lying across the path face up, back resting against a tree. Despite the mask hiding his mouth she can see that he is very pale. A fleeting thought paralyses her: the virus killed him! Our sick joke of a government has failed to tell us it's mutated. People are now dropping dead where they stand.

Shaking away the notion she moves closer, up to the 2 metre limit. He looks young. She can't tell if he is breathing or not and doesn't want to touch him. There's no smell of alcohol. Then she sees the blood, it's pooling and drying around his t-shirt collar. Without thinking she reaches for her mobile, dials 999, hesitates at the question then says, "Ambulance."

The reception down here is shit but a calm woman tells her to describe the exact location, instructs not to attempt mouth to mouth, starts to talk her through what to do, tells her to stay on the line. Then the signal cuts out. No amount of phone waving will get it to reconnect. Someone appears at the end of the long avenue. The mobile juggling transforms into an attempt to catch their attention. Feeling foolish she shouts, "Help!"

The figure turns and starts walking towards them.

Glancing down at the body hoping for some change, she looks up again and a tall man, overdressed in a heavy black overcoat, is standing next to her. He must have run but doesn't appear to be panting. It's difficult to tell because of his mask. It's made out of a scarlet material. Set against his dark hair and clothing it resembles a vivid slash across his face. He's standing too close and she takes a step back.

"Found him five minutes ago. I've called an ambulance."

The man peers at a large, expensive-looking watch.

"They will be too late."

He's definitely not local. He pronounces each word carefully as if relishing their individual sounds rather than trying to form them into a sentence.

"I don't know if he's alive or dead," she says.

The eyes above the mask crinkle as if reacting to something amusing.

"No, it is sometimes difficult to tell."

The relief she felt at his appearance is turning to anger and alarm. The weight of the pepper spray in her jacket pocket is reassuring.

"Do you think we should cover him up?" She looks meaningfully at his coat. Ignoring the hint the man slowly wags his finger and says, "No."

Putting his head on one side he starts speaking as if they were old friends who had bumped into each other, rather than two strangers with a body on the ground between them.

"I presume all this . . . " and his wrist traces a circle in the air, ". . . must seem to you strange, extraordinary even. I have seen it all before. Plague, influenza, the Black Death. Oh my, that was a time. A happy one for us. Almost as good as a war. It makes your kind distracted, isolated, vulnerable."

Nodding to himself he moves towards her. "What is it they say? Make hay . . . although the second half of that saying definitely does not apply."

Pulling out the aerosol, she holds it an arm's length in front of her.

"Stay back! The police will be here soon."

He tugs down his mask revealing lean, handsome features and a pitying, self-satisfied smile.

"Yes, no doubt, but too late for you, my dear."

The spray hits him directly in the eyes. He doesn't

blink as it collects on his skin and runs down his cheeks. The sardonic smile widens so that she can now see the razor-sharp fangs at the sides of his mouth. With amazing speed, his hand closes around her throat. It feels like a band of iron. His face is transformed, animalistic. The jaw opens impossibly wide and stoops toward the pulsing artery in her neck. Her left hand goes limp and the spent can drops to the floor. The right strikes forward with practised strength and precision.

"Have you seen this before, fucker?"

There is time for a brief flash of surprise as he stares down at the wooden stake sticking from his chest. A scream begins in his throat but then the air crackles as he burns and falls into a heap of ash. She steps back, to avoid the flames but also to savour his fleeting look of terror. Some small recompense for all the pain the murdering bastard had caused.

Kicking the stake clear of the smouldering pile she picks it up and blows off some embers. Made from an exotic South American hardwood, notches have been painstakingly scrapped into the handle. Now another will be added.

A siren blares through the dusk. She gazes down at the corpse of the young man. "I'm sorry I was too late to save you, brother."

Her eyes narrow and the muscles beneath them spasm

as she looks up at the path ahead. "I can't save you all."

Putting away the tools of her trade she sets out again on her vigil, her vocation, her endless mission.

Sophie
By Dorothy Cox

The first time I see her she is walking along the canal towpath. I haven't been looking for her. She arrives in my life. That's just how it is. No fanfares or fireworks, but I know she is the one. I follow her carefully, quietly along the path. She crosses the bridge. I follow her to the block of flats at the end of the road. I am glad I have my camera.

The second time I see her we bump into each other in the shop doorway. I am on my way back from my lunch break. She is leaving after buying a book.

"Oh, I'm sorry," we say, in unison, stooping down together to retrieve the book she has dropped. She laughs. A golden, beautiful laugh. She is so beautiful.

"Thank you," she says, and is gone.

I have to see her again. My job at the bookshop is only part-time; just two days a week and extra if any of the permanent staff are ill or on holiday. It isn't ideal, but beggars can't be choosers. They tell me I am lucky to have a job at all.

"Quite a looker, she is," says my colleague who had witnessed our collision. "She's ordered another book. Studying English Lit at Uni."

I snatch a glimpse of his computer screen as he completes the order. Sophie Bennett. She's going to call on Friday morning to pick up the book. There is a mobile number too. I memorise it. I phone it twice over the next few days just to hear her voice but cut the call.

No doubt my acquaintances would tell you I have few virtues, but I am a patient man. Friday morning finds me sitting in a café across the market square from the bookshop, an unimpeded view of the entrance, my camera in my pocket. I know she will come. Just as I finish my coffee, there she is. I watch her enter the shop.

After leaving the bookshop she goes straight into the bakery next door, emerging minutes later, croissant in hand. She wanders along the rows of market stalls set up in the square. She buys apples and a CD. I have no trouble keeping her in view. Her red duffel coat and multicoloured scarf stand out from the drab surroundings.

I watch her leave the square and walk up the hill towards the university. Her figure becomes smaller as she draws away from me. Reaching the top, she disappears through the gates.

I guess that lectures will keep her there for the rest of the day. At 4 o'clock I station myself just inside the entrance gates, confident that I will see her leave. The wait is in vain. By 5 o'clock the whole campus is deserted. Of course, it is Friday. Everyone leaves early.

The whole weekend is frustrating and miserable. I am either wandering around town hoping that I might see her somewhere, or just sitting in my room. With the photographs. It's work all day on Monday and Tuesday. By Wednesday I am beginning to feel desperate. But wasn't it Wednesday that she had come into the shop? I assume that she will have lectures today.

I walk up the hill to the university entrance. In front of the main building is a courtyard, with a rather tired fountain. The water spits out intermittently, dribbling down the moss-covered stem to the grubby pool at its base. There are hard concrete benches all around the courtyard and I choose a bench with a good view furthest away from the main doors.

Mid-afternoon she emerges with a group of students, laughing and joking. My patience is rewarded. I slide the camera from my pocket. They turn to walk further up the hill. Is she going with them? I stand up and then, with relief, I see her turn and head off down the hill to the square. Lectures are obviously over for the day.

She hurries straight across the square and crosses the

road to the bus stop. A bus comes along. I make a note of the number 31. I know the 31 bus will not take her home and when it pulls away Sophie is still at the stop. She boards the next one and I see the flash of her red coat as she moves along the bus. Number 63.

Over the next few days I spend hours waiting outside the university, hoping I will see her. I must see her. I grow increasingly frustrated. I even try phoning again. When she picks up I say nothing.

Finally, this evening, as I leave the book shop, I see her coming into the square, heading for the bus stop. I turn and run as fast as I can across the main road and past the bus stop. I need to get to the stop before the one where she gets on. I need to be on the bus when she gets on it. Sweating with the effort and wet from the increasing drizzle, I cover the half mile to the bus stop just as the number 63 pulls up. I sit at the back. And yes, there she is, at the next stop.

She gets on and shows the driver her bus pass. He says something and she smiles at him. I want to scream at him. I grip the rail on the back of the seat in front of me so hard my knuckles are white. She sits in front of me about halfway back, just behind the middle door.

Now I have time to study her closely. She is so beautiful. The photos don't do her justice. I can only see her back at the moment but of course, I saw her face again as she got on the bus. She hasn't noticed me. Why should she? She doesn't seem to notice any of the passengers. She is reading a book now. Looking down, her long dark hair falls either side of her face. My last girl had dark hair too, not long but short and curly. She was a waitress in a coffee shop, not really my type at all. I know Sophie is the one I have been waiting for for so long. She is exactly right. I move forward and slide into the seat just behind her. I am close enough to breathe in the scent from her hair.

She is wearing her red duffel coat, and the long, long multi-coloured scarf is wrapped around her neck. I guess at her height. 5ft 5? 5ft 6? A couple of inches shorter than me, anyway. She is slim too, I am sure. I imagine her without the coat and scarf, imagine her taking them off . . .

On the empty seat beside her there is a hessian bag with some green message on it that I haven't been able to read. What has she got in it? Books perhaps? Does she have work to do at home?

Can she sense my stare? I feel that strong connection, that spark, that familiar sensation. I felt it as soon as I saw her that day in the bookshop and I realised that I had seen her before that, yes, that day on the towpath. Surely she can feel it too. She must.

She brushes her hair out of her eyes and over her shoulder, over the coils of the scarf. It almost brushes my face. The faint scent that wafts towards me is something flowery. Her hair shines. As she tucks a strand of hair behind her ear, I see her hand. Small, no rings, and short, perfect nails. Her coat sleeve falls back a little and there's a delicate silver watch round her perfect, narrow wrist.

I know she will get off the bus close to the park. I glance out of the grimy window. It is dark now and the grey drizzle of the afternoon has left everything damp. The bus is almost at the end of its run and we are the only two passengers left. She is so engrossed in her book I don't think she knows I am here.

She looks up suddenly, it must be her stop next. She drops the book into her bag and scrambles to the door. The bus pulls in, I wait until the doors open then I stand up too. And follow.

She steps off and turns to the left. She moves off quickly. I pull my coat collar up against the chill and damp. I wait a moment and follow, just far enough behind to keep her in sight. She turns off the lane down the unlit alleyway towards the park and the canal towpath. And I follow. I know she is the one . . .

The Old Man in the Tree
By Maureen Taylor

The start of the day was easy in the very first moment. Then one by one my cares and worries also began to wake from the forgetfulness of sleep and started to cling and weigh me down. What usually helped at this time was my first look out into the garden. There was always something comforting to see: the progress of the spring shoots and the birds flitting back and forth, picking through the dead leaves for grubs. The longtails usually came to the feeder at the same time in the morning; I had grown attached to them and didn't want to miss them, however dreadful those waking moments had been.

On that particular day, as I drew open the curtains, the patch of winter irises caught my eye; they seemed to have crept up without me noticing them. I scanned the garden to see what else was going on. Along with the birds, there was an old man sitting quietly on the biggest branch of the ash tree. He wasn't there when I went to bed so I really don't know when he arrived. He seemed to be quite settled, resting his back against the trunk. His arms were folded and his hands tucked into the wide sleeves of his full grey robe. Still, I thought he might be feeling the chill with just his sandals on so I went out to ask if he wanted a hot drink or something to eat. He smiled and said, "Thank you. I am well."

The old man seemed quite content and I was sure that when he was ready, he would pick up his journey to wherever he was going. I went about my usual routine and when I was walking back from the shop with the newspaper, I met Mr Boyle from around the corner. He was so pleased to hear about the old man in my tree. "It's good to hear he's still around. We would miss him if he stopped coming," he said.

I wondered how I had never heard of the old man before. His presence was clearly welcomed by some, and I began to feel quite privileged that he had decided to settle down with me for a while. This was the first time I had felt important to anyone in a long time. It was a nice feeling.

I was glad to see the old man was still in the tree when I got back home but Mr Ford, the man next door, was obviously not so keen to have him around. "You can't let him stay there all day. He's mad," he said. Without waiting for a response he stomped back into his house huffing and puffing. It was all rather confusing given that Mr Boyle had spoken so warmly of our visitor.

On balance, I decided, the old man wasn't causing any harm. He probably just needed a rest and he would be on his way again soon. And I felt a little pleased with myself for not just deferring to Mr Ford, even if I wasn't able to think of a clever reply just at that moment. I called up to the old man in the tree, "Don't worry. You are welcome to stay. I am just inside. Let me know if you need anything."

"Thank you," he said. "I am well."

With no other company, and nothing much else to do that day, I decided to sit by the window with my sewing to keep a watchful eye on the old man. He seemed to be quite comfortable, but I was worried he could get tired as the day went on and his position on the branch might become more precarious.

Part of me wanted him to stay and I didn't want him to leave without the chance to say goodbye. Throughout the day I offered him cups of tea. A sandwich. A cushion. Each was declined by the old man, saying, "Thank you. I am well."

It was nice to have something else to think about, and the presence of the old man seemed to bring a sense of peace that I had not felt in a while. The longer he was there, the more I began to think that this wasn't just a chance stop in a convenient place. It felt like he was as concerned about me as I was about him.

As the afternoon wore on, I turned momentarily to my pattern and when I looked out again the old man was gone. I was so upset I hadn't seen him go and I rushed out into the garden, hoping that he might just have gone for a walk around. He was nowhere to be seen, but the sinking sense of loss that began to prick my eyes was quickly overcome by the warm breeze that wrapped around me.

I looked up and caught sight of a large grey bird circling high above. I closed my eyes and stretched out my arms. It felt like all my concerns and worries were being drawn away towards the bird in the sky, dissipating in the air. I was able to breathe more easily than I had in a long time. I signalled to the bird and whispered, "Thank you. I am well."

Cody's Escape
By Tony Oswick

Cody left before I woke. The poor guy was scared outta his wits, scared like a white-tailed deer in a forest fire. He knew Fender was sniffing around looking for him, knew he was on his tail.

The town was in uproar last night. There was evil in the air – is every Friday when Fender and the Pariahs hit the streets. Them Pariahs are no weekend warriors, they're genuine one-hundred-percenters. Someone said three young kids from Lornsburg got knifed.

Me and Cody was okay up here in the motel but it was only a matter of time before Fender tracked him down. He knew Cody was the one who'd grassed him up.

"You're the only thing that keeps me sane, babe," Cody told me last night. "I'll call you when it's safe, when Fender's off the scent. I loves you Lorrie-Jo, you knows that."

"You just saying that Cody Brame? Just 'cos you needs a place to hide tonight?" He didn't say a thing, just held me tighter. I wanted to believe him.

Later while we was lying quiet in bed he told me he'd be going before sun-up. "I gotta get out of this hell-hole. If Fender finds me, you knows what he'll do. Same as he did to Fox Bevan." He drew a finger across his neck. Everyone knew about Fox Bevan. They said the blood seeped to every corner of the room before he died.

"Where you gonna hide? That Fender's a mean polecat."

Then he told me his screwball plan. "You can't do it, Cody, it's a damned crazy notion," I said. "How you gonna get away without your bike? Fender'll catch up with you easy. Anyways, how many hours of slaving in the gas station did that bike cost you? It's precious." *More precious than me*, I thought, but didn't say.

He nodded. "I knows, babe. But I been thinking hard and it's the only way. Fender ain't no brainbox. He'll believe it. Then he won't be chasing anymore and you and me can get as far away from this place as ever we want."

I dozed on and off, thinking about what Cody had said. I must've gone to sleep about half-two 'cos when I woke he was gone, just like he said. The bed was still warm. I didn't hear him go, not even the noise of his precious bike.

...

I was back on duty at eight and The Pariahs came calling at the motel just after ten. This guy, all grease and leather-jacket, barged in as though he owned the place. I'd never seen him before but I knew it was Fender.

He leaned through the hatch. "You seen a jerk named Cody Brame? Rides a Victory 8-Ball. Red-faced, tattoo of a rattle-snake on his neck, mean-looking turkey."

Not as mean-looking as you, I thought. "Cody Brame? Why, he's been through here this very morning. Left on the Tularosa road not more than an hour past. Said he was heading for Bingham." It was what Cody told me to say.

"Looked kinda drugged out, though. Told him he shouldn't be riding. Not in that state, not if he was going to Bingham through Otter Creek Canyon. Know what I mean?"

He took me by my chin. "I know what you mean, sweet-cheeks. I bet you're a real good girl." He glanced at my badge and eyed my sweater.

"Yeah young Lorrie-Jo, if you're lucky, I may come back to thank you properly." I could smell his rank breath. As his hand dropped from my chin, it brushed against my breasts.

I ignored him. Cody told me how Fender treated his women. I didn't want to end up scarred.

I watched Fender and his gang head off down the Tularosa road in a cloud of dust, their bikes geared to wake anyone still sleeping in the motel. It'd take less than twenty minutes for them to get to Otter Creek Canyon. That's where Cody said he was gonna do it, the fool-ass of a man.

"I'll hang out at Otter Creek. When I hear Fender coming, I'll send the bike over the edge," he told me last night. "The river runs narrow down there and the bike'll burst into flames where all them rocks are. Create a firestorm. Fender'll think I've gone over as well."

"But ain't that over-dramatic?" I protested.

"Fender knows how much I loves that bike. He'll never believe I'd trash it deliberately." Cody hesitated. "But if it saves my life?" He smiled for the first time that night.

I was still in the motel office when I heard Fender and his gang racing back into town. They didn't bother to stop by. Guess they'd seen Cody's bike trashed and fired at the bottom of Otter Creek, and supposed Cody was there too, his body burnt to a cinder. Perhaps his plan had worked after all?

It's nine now and the sun'll be going down soon. The folks at the motel have been full of the accident at Otter Creek. Some even went to rubberneck at the charred remains of Cody's bike.

I'm still waiting for him to call. I ain't heard a single peep from him. Cody said not to ring but I've tried anyways. I had to, but he ain't answering. Why don't that crazy buzzard let me know he's okay?

I tells you, there's a fear creeping all over me. Cody was acting kinda strange last night, real strange. I need to be certain he did what he said he was gonna do, be certain he wants to stay alive, be certain he wants to be with me. But there's this nagging doubt.

And he never said goodbye.

Life in Lines
By Linda Hurdwell

The sky is blue with a few scudding clouds. It looks a nice day. Hilary thinks about going out. She hasn't been outside for ten weeks. The time is almost 11.30am so, if she is going, she must go soon.

Suddenly she leaps up from the sofa, puts on her blue jacket and nervously opens the front door. She peers down the street. Empty, that's good. She steps forward and slamming the door behind her, strides along until she arrives at the crossroads. Few cars are about. That is also good.

Turning to her left, Hilary makes her way to the park. Walking straight, but avoiding any cracks, she arrives at the pond. Hilary decides it is not large enough to be a lake, so it must be a pond. A good place to sit for a while, and she plonks down on the nearest park bench, realising she is quite breathless. It has been a long time since she has walked so far and her sturdy body is almost in pain with the exertion. She feels shaky.

She glances at her watch and sees it isn't even midday yet, so it didn't take her as long as she'd anticipated. A man is approaching, tall, lanky, about her age. She prays he won't stop, she isn't ready to speak to a man, but he stops right beside her, frowning for a moment. Her large body is sitting right in the middle of the bench, but he plops down beside her on the left. Their bodies are not touching.

"I have to sit here," he blurts out. "I have walked exactly three miles so now I must rest."

She merely nods. He is staring at the ducks, and suddenly jumps up glaring at them.

"There are five mallards, but there should be six." Then he sits next to her again. "I used to call them ducks with green helmets, but I know now their name is a mallard."

She shyly peers at him then hides her face in her hands. She shrugs, and produces a large cheese sandwich from her jacket pocket and begins to eat, one of her favourite occupations.

The man is still staring at the ducks. "They need some of your bread," he says. "Can you spare some, please?"

Sighing, she breaks some off and hands it to the man who stands again to throw it to the ducks. "There it is." He grins. She looks unsure. "The sixth mallard. Look, flying over for some food."

They both watch intently as the duck swims across the pond. Rather beautiful to see. But she must return home now, before things become complicated. This man is beginning to make her nervous, but he suddenly grabs her wrist.

"Who are you, what is your name?"

Her voice is a whisper. "Hilary."

He sits down beside her again and laughs. "I can call you Hill, then, there are no ovals. Just straight lines, like my name, Will."

"Oh." Hilary is confused and then looking at her watch she sees it is almost 12.30. They sit in silence until Hilary heaves herself up and attempts to ease her wrist from his clutches.

"I have to go home now."

"Why?"

"My mother needs me."

He stands too, adding, "Hill, we can walk back together, but you must miss the cracks, I don't like to walk on cracks in the paths."

"Neither do I," she laughs and as he lets go of her wrist, they stroll back. Hilary is surprised at how comfortable she feels beside him. She glances up at him, noting his thick unruly dark hair, a bit like hers, and piercing blue eyes. That should be unnerving, but it isn't.

He is a bit odd, but so is she. Or so she's been told. Their steps are in time. He says very little and she likes that.

"Hill," he speaks at the park entrance now. "We can do this again tomorrow."

"Okay Will." She turns to her right and he turns to the left. Hilary makes her way back home and almost skips with a lighter step.

The following day they meet, and slowly speak a little more. He lives in a flat alone and is almost 40, exactly like herself. They meet every day, until one morning it is raining, absolutely teeming. Now what should she do? Not go? But she has the urge to meet him, which is strange. She hasn't spoken to another human being since her mother left her.

At 11.30 on the dot, Hilary dons her blue mac, and holding her blue umbrella leaves home heading for the park. She likes the colour blue. She hasn't got any boots and her blue shoes are letting in the water, some is trickling down her neck. Yet she strides, as fast as she can to the park and stands beside the bench. It's too wet to sit on.

She droops, feeling suddenly forlorn and silly. He won't come, she feels sure, and decides to return home with a sinking feeling. She wants to cry. But, he is coming, loping up to her and holding a large plastic cover.

They hardly look at each other but when he lays the cover onto the bench, they both sit down, and she still has her umbrella up so they won't get too wet.

"It's raining heavily," she murmurs more to herself, but he replies.

"Yes. Approximately one thousand drops each second. The ducks don't feel it. They have extra body fat to keep them warm on days like this.

She giggles.

"You know a lot. When I met you I hadn't been out of the house for over a two months."

Will said nothing at first then admitted, "I walk for exactly three miles each day to keep fit. At home I draw and look on my computer to learn things and I clean the rooms every other day." He speaks without taking a breath before adding, "What about you, Hill?"

She sighs. What does she do? She thinks of the unmade bed, the pile of unwashed dishes in the sink and the dirty clothes in the bathroom.

"Before, I went everywhere with my mum, but she died of a heart attack, right in front of me." Tears spill from her eyes. "I screamed and screamed. A neighbour called an ambulance and they took her away. Now I sit and stare out of the window. I don't like talking to other people, I like being on my own."

"Why is that Hill?"

"I just liked it talking to Mum."

"But you said she was dead."

"I can still speak to her."

Will nods. "I understand. I never knew my mother, but I might miss her if I had. I tried going to work but that was no good. The people found me odd, they said."

"Me too. People never liked me."

"I understand."

Then, simultaneously they both stand leaving the bench and he carefully folds up the plastic sheet and carries it with him. They say very little now as they are concentrating on missing the cracks in the path. Suddenly at the entrance Will stops and grabs her wrist.

"When we first met you told me a lie."

She trembles. "Did I? What makes you think that?"

"You said you had to go home because your mum needs you, but she is dead."

Hilary doesn't answer and Will lets go of her wrist.

"But Hill, I understand, you still need to talk to her."

Wiping the rain from his face he adds, "How do you buy food, you love eating?"

"A support worker does it for me, leaves it on the doorstep. I haven't talked to her yet, I just smile at her through the window. I don't let her in."

"Maybe you will one day."

She nods, and even though his dark hair is flat and wet, clinging to his thin, serious face, he looks nice.

She giggles. "You look like a drowned rat," and Will laughs.

"So do you." Then as they reach the park entrance he leans over and kisses her nose. "Your nose is like a big long raindrop." For a second their hands touch, then quickly part.

"Look Hill, we have a rainbow and from here it appears straight." He is staring up at the sky.

"Goodbye, Hill." He kisses her wet nose again.

He leaves her standing there feeling flustered and rather excited. He kissed her. Twice.

She turns to go home and decides that today she might not have time to talk to her mum. She wants to wash the dishes and think about being kissed.

Judgement Day
By Kevin Sleight

"Has the jury reached a verdict on which you are all agreed?"

The heat in the courtroom was stifling. The air hung there as if it had just solidified and the smallest movement was an effort. Suits and dresses stuck like damp sponges to the bodies of the men and women who, in the main, would rather be somewhere else.

I tried to remain calm. But I found myself asking the same question I had asked myself over and over again these past few weeks. How had I gotten into this mess in the first place?

I'll tell you now, because when all's said and done, it's pretty straightforward really. Murder usually is. No need to complicate things. This isn't Agatha Christie, although my story comes with all the usual ingredients. A dead body. Female. A prime suspect – me, of course. A weapon. A bread knife – with my fingerprints on the handle. Stupid really. But shock is hardly conducive to rational behaviour.

A motive? Yes. And to cap it all, a police department with too many crimes to solve and no real interest in checking beyond the obvious. Averse to looking a gift horse in the mouth they were not. But I'm getting ahead of myself. So permit me to backtrack a little.

My name is William Gibson. I'm married to Danielle who I love, have two kids – one boy, one girl – both grown and flown the proverbial nest. I make a fair pot of money helping big corporations swallow up small corporations. More or less the perfect lifestyle, you might think. And you'd be right. In principle.

Enter Jackie.

Jackie is, or rather was, the natural consequence of an all-too-human weakness for a varied diet. A hooker, in point of fact. Not your everyday street-corner variety. Nice, presentable, sexy naturally, intelligent even. And affordable. She had her own convenient direct-access apartment in a renovated warehouse in what realtors like to describe as an 'up-and-coming neighborhood'.

I'd been buying what Jackie had to sell for the better part of six months. Not too often, just often enough to scratch the occasional itch.

Truth be told, I liked her a lot. And within the confines of a strictly business 'relationship', I believe she liked me.

So why would I kill her?

Four months have passed since the good times came to an abrupt halt, but I can see her now as if it were only yesterday. Lying on the floor, almost naked, the knife sticking out of her chest, blood everywhere.

I'd turned up as arranged at 8 o'clock in the evening. I was supposed to be 'networking' with a 'business associate'.

I should have realised immediately something was wrong when her front door was open. I nearly fainted when I saw her in her satin and lace boudoir.

My first instincts were to run, get the hell out. I'd already half turned away. Then Jackie groaned; a low, throaty near-death cry for help.

I did what seemed the right thing to do and knelt before her, cradling her head in my arms. Never thought to call an ambulance. Soon found out that it would have made no difference.

She tried to speak. Failed. Tried again. Whispered something, a single word. "Judge . . . ment." Then she died.

I left her where I'd found her.

Out in the street, sweating, nearly hyperventilating, I caught myself saying, "I will Jackie, I will . . ."

Stupid. Who did I think I was? Sherlock Holmes? Columbo? What chance did I have of finding her killer? I'd be lucky if the police didn't come knocking on my door, asking me the awkward questions I'd have asked the prime suspect if I found one. Needless to say, I wasn't lucky.

My fingerprints were on the murder weapon and they were already on file – dating back to when I was young and free and stupid and caught in possession of a controlled substance. I was traced in the time it took a hard drive to search the relevant database: no time at all.

Had I touched the knife? Clearly I had.

Had I been in the vicinity of Jackie's flat around the time of her death? The closed circuit camera in the gas station I stopped at, less than a mile from her apartment, said I had.

And the 8 o'clock entry in her diary that said simply **W** further tightened the proverbial noose around my neck.

Naturally I pleaded my innocence because I was innocent. Naturally I hired the best attorney my money could buy. Naturally I went with the flow when Danielle said she wanted a divorce. What else could I do?

And to my eternal shame, in the quagmire of my misery, I forgot about my promise to Jackie, "I will Jackie, I will . . ." In my defence, the thought of ten thousand volts of electricity or a lethal injection surging through one's body can be somewhat distracting.

"We have."

"And do you find the defendant guilty or not guilty?"

"We find the defendant . . ."

It must have been the third week of the trial when the penny dropped. I was sitting where I always sat, doodling on the legal pad in front of me. My very expensive attorney was cross-questioning one of the arresting officers, and to my mind not doing a particularly good job of it.

It was the diary that gave me that lightbulb moment.

"Oh, Jackie. I understand."

At first I couldn't believe it. What I was thinking was preposterous.

Then I thought about it a bit more. She was picky, I knew that. And after 'business' she liked to talk about her customers. No names, mind. Hookers are like attorneys. Client confidentiality is everything. But having established the ground rule – no names, no pack drill – a bit of titillating hot-gossip didn't go amiss. In particular, she talked about someone a little bit special. A new client. Someone going places. About to make a name for himself.

The 6 o'clock client surely. Never identified. He was there in black-and-white anonymity in the prosecution's Exhibit 17, being the relevant page of Jackie's diary. Right there above me, the untraceable **P** above my slam-dunked **W**.

My mind flashed back to Jackie's apartment that evening. **P** was there for his 6 o'clock appointment. Something was going wrong. Had she decided he was worth more than the usual hourly rate? Had greed overcome caution? Had the reality of what he was doing and how vulnerable he was suddenly hit home like a bullet to the chest?

Knowing what I knew of her, I tried to picture it. Yes, it was a stretch, but nothing else made sense. Greed is a powerful emotion. And in some of us, the veneer of respectability is wafer thin. The more I thought about it, the more convinced I became. She'd chosen the wrong guy to up the ante. Or the guy decided the ante was already too high for his liking.

All of a sudden 2 plus 2 made exactly 4. At least in my somewhat fevered, desperate mind it did. Not that it would do me any good.

Who would believe me? And would it make any difference?

At this stage in the trial, it was all down to the jury.

What did they see when they looked at me? A fat cat that needed cutting down to size? A fiend who'd ruthlessly murdered a woman fallen from grace? Or a basically decent guy who just happened to have strayed from the nest and found himself in the wrong place at the wrong time?

Roll the dice.

. . .

". . . guilty or not guilty?"

Finally it was time. After nearly a month of trial and two day's deliberation – the jury had reached its verdict.

I stood up as bidden. The foreman of the jury stood also.

Had the members of the jury reached a verdict on which they were all agreed?

They had.

I closed my eyes.

I listened to the foreman's voice.

As did the man facing me. The man who the smart money said would be the next appointee to the US Supreme Court.

The man with everything to lose.

Judge Peter Mentoni.

Six-o-clock Peter.

Judge Ment . . . oni.

"Guilty."

Harry's Chair
By Cathy Ives

Vera sits in the only chair left in the house; it's Harry's chair. Furniture has been disappearing for a while now. The settee has gone and so has the china cabinet, her dressing table and wardrobe.

All that's left in her bedroom is her bed. She knows this for certain because she got out of it this morning feeling all hot and bothered. There are a couple of boxes and some black bags which she thinks belong to her but she isn't entirely sure.

She was going somewhere – her son Robert had told her this on several occasions. Where or why she was going she didn't know. But she wouldn't need her furniture, Robert had said. Just her clothes and a few odds and ends; some keepsakes, photos, favourite books, letters, that sort of thing. It was a shame about the furniture, she'd had some of it for as far back as she could remember.

And she can remember quite a way back.

It was all bought and paid for, the furniture. Harry was very strict about that. "Can't have what we can't pay for, gal." He was always saying that. So everything had been collected bit by bit, as they could afford it. They would go out on Saturday afternoons and mooch around the junk shops looking for what they needed and then Harry would haggle with the owner for a bargain. Lucky they had that old van Harry used for his painting and decorating. It was pretty clapped-out but it got them places. When they got home Vera would have to help him unload. Didn't matter what it was – a table, a chair, a bed – she had to put her back into it and lift.

Vera and Harry had married right after he was demobbed; in the registry office, church wasn't for them. There he stood in his shiny demob suit with his mate Ernie as his witness and her in her best frock, carrying a bunch of daisies. Ida her sister was her witness. Then it was home to her mum and dad's for their wedding tea. Food was on ration but someone had managed to find a tin of salmon and a tin of peaches from somewhere.

From that day on they had hardly ever been apart except when Harry was working – and he worked hard, bless him. Vera worked too, part-time in a sweet shop, and when she wasn't at work she was keeping the house clean, sewing and mending or getting Harry's dinner ready. On the rare occasions they went out of an evening they would always go together. Harry's never been one for going down the pub and leaving Vera at home.

She called out to him now but there was just silence. Thinking about it, she hadn't seen him at all lately. He was probably in his greenhouse. He did spend a lot of time in there but it was about time he showed his face. He had always grown his own veg. "Saves paying for it, eh, gal."

Vera shifts in Harry's chair. No one dares sit in it unless he's out, not even Vera. She had shouted at Robert when he had suggested taking it away. She told him straight that it was staying put and anyway, she wouldn't want to be in his shoes if Harry found it gone.

By the side of the chair is her big brown handbag. She picks it up, it's heavy. Harry had bought it for her on a day out in Clacton, or was it Margate? It could have been Frinton. She opens the large clasp, there is everything in it: lipstick, powder compact, letters and old black-and-white photographs, her manicure set in its leather case – a birthday present from Robert when he was little; chose it himself, Harry had said. There were spare glasses and keys for she didn't know what.

She rummages around and pulls out a bundle of letters, mostly from Harry when he was overseas. Then she gets out a photograph of him all dressed up in his army uniform. She never tired of looking at him so smart;

and that smile that made him even more good looking. No wonder she fell for him.

"Didn't have a chance did I, you ole' charmer," she says out loud. There aren't tears in her eyes, she doesn't need her hankie. She puts the things back in the bag and clasps it shut, her big sturdy bag. It goes everywhere with her, wherever she's going.

See You at Twilight
By Michael Downes

He stood in the crowded aisle, clutching a support pole while the train swayed, picking up speed between stations. In 20 minutes he would be home with her again. Twenty minutes. At work all he ever did now was count down the hours to when he would speak to her again.

He recalled, as he always did on his journey home, how they met. She was out jogging when she twisted her ankle and stopped at a park bench to assess the damage. He was there purely by chance. He had never before entered the park.

From that chance meeting a magnificent romance blossomed that neither of them anticipated. Within six months they were married – no formalities such as an engagement were necessary which shocked their friends. But they both knew that what they shared was something very special, sacred even, and they pitied those who would never come to understand the sheer joy they felt in each other's company.

They had found each other – he 51, she 45, both with professional jobs; he an executive director of a large nationwide retail company, she an interior designer with her own expanding company. On their first anniversary he bought her a luxury car. She maintained it was too robust compared to her modest little hatchback, and hardly ever drove it unless the hatchback was being serviced.

The train began to slow down; the next station coming up was his. He stood by the door waiting for it to slide open, and once it did he was one of the first out on the platform. He hurried along, and almost ran to a waiting taxi and into the back seat. Five minutes later the cab stopped outside the luxury apartment complex overlooking the bay. He punched in his personal code and entered the premises. An elevator took him to the twentieth floor. He stepped out and headed for door 2044. Before he swiped his card to unlock it he paused for a moment. He thought of all the things he would say to her, the very same words he had been saying every evening for the past four months. He knew those words so well, like a well-rehearsed script. He swiped and entered.

"I'm home, darling. How was your day?"

There was no reply. He went to the fridge, took out a

beer and poured it into a highball glass, all the while as if in conversation with someone.

"Whoops . . . almost forgot, honey." He took the last bottle of cabernet from the wine rack and opened it. As he half-filled the wine glass, he said, "Come and get it, darling. In the kitchen waiting for you!"

He sat on the sofa she had designed and let his eyes around wander the spacious living area. Everything in it had her signature. Directly across from him was a large glass-plated sliding door which led out to the balcony, now locked, the key having been thrown away months ago. A long coffee table lay in front like a barrier, stacked with all her books and magazines.

To his left was a feature wall and hanging from it was a life-size poster of her. He raised his glass and saluted it. He looked back at the sliding door and wondered what it would feel like to jump from it, arms and legs outstretched like a base jumper. But not from the twentieth, no, from the thirtieth. Much more dramatic.

His musings led him to the accident. Two youths in a stolen car ran a red light smashing side on into the hatchback. It was a miracle she survived: a twisted spine, smashed pelvis, and a suppressed rib cage, among other injuries. He finished his beer and decided to make himself a light meal.

"Your wine is going to taste stale, Robyn, if you don't

show yourself soon." He picked it up and took a sip, then another. "Hmm . . . you certainly have good taste, honey, certainly know your wines."

He sipped at it again and placed it out of reach as he prepared his meal, and as he did he sang. He sang all her favourite songs, one after the other. She always said he had a fine tenor voice and should have used it as a profession. He laughed out loud. "And how in heaven's name, woman, would I have met you!"

Later he showered again with the bathroom door ajar. He had good reason for doing this, because only a few days ago someone had entered while he showered and then left again. He couldn't be sure if it was her, but it couldn't have been anyone else. And now as the water sprayed over him he kept an eye on the door. Through the foggy glass he could make out the dark outline of someone.

"Robyn!"

He jumped out and flung the door opened. "I know you're here!" He ran into the living room, then the bedroom and the spare room. He searched everywhere. "I saw you, girl. You can't fool me!"

He sat down in defeat on the sofa, dripping wet, naked.

"I saw you . . . I saw you." His words quivered. He put his hands over his face and lay down curled up in the foetal position muttering until sleep came upon him.

At around midnight he woke and made his way to his bedroom. There he got into his pyjamas and laid out her nightgown across the bottom of the bed, just as he did every night with the bedroom door open. "Just in case you wish to sleep with me," he said.

In the morning he rose and showered with the door ajar, but he didn't see her. He made coffee and toast and sat at the breakfast bar. Then he drank the rest of her wine, washed the glass and put it away. All was quiet. When he was ready to leave he picked up his coat and announced, "I'm off Robyn."

He made for the door, and as he was about to open it he stopped. This was the moment he faced every day since the accident, and he dreaded it as much as he looked forward to it. He could hear her, her supreme effort to reach him. He turned to face her. Her sunken eyes were wide open, fighting back the pain that was always there, her disfigured face once so lovely, now a hollow grey mask. She collapsed into him. He held her in his arms. He could smell her fragrance, her breath on his cheek, and her final words that morning, "See you at twilight."

And just like every morning he felt numb and wrecked with guilt, and asking himself: why did he leave her alone that fateful morning. And then, as suddenly as she was in his arms, she was gone . . . gone again until the same time tomorrow. He let his arms drop, turned round and left the apartment.

He waited for the elevator. It arrived within minutes, half full. As he rode it down to the ground floor, he looked up at the unlit button of level thirty. He had never been there, but he promised himself one day he would.

The elevator doors opened at the ground floor. Everyone left, except him. He kept staring up at the thirtieth, and then saw himself press the button that would take him there. The elevator seemed to fly as it soared towards its destination. He felt a quickening, an excitement. He put on his coat. He could visualise standing on the ledge, his coat flapping up around him, his arms and legs outstretched and his last words the same as hers, "See you at twilight."

Amid the Winter Snow
By Donovan Laurie

The train which had crept in fits and starts from Charing Cross came to a sudden halt. In Coach Three, the lights flickered and went out, to subdued expressions of alarm. Then they came on again, to audible sighs of relief.

Yesterday's news had warned of snow and ice, and disruption to train services.

In a seat at the front of the coach, a blond-haired girl gave a little cry and put her hands on her swollen stomach.

"Are you okay, Maria?" The thin-faced youth in jeans and hoodie sitting opposite asked anxiously.

"I'm alright, Joe," she replied a little breathlessly. "At least I think so!"

The man in the seat behind leaned over his wife, and the two Selfridges' bags in front of her, and peered out of the window.

"We're stuck in a tunnel," he said, and turning his

head, looked up at the sign above the door *The Next Station is Orpington*.

There was another cry from the girl in the front seat.

"Joe! I think the baby's coming!"

"It can't be, Maria. There's over a month to go," he said desperately.

"I don't know, Joe." She gave another cry. "I'm sure it's on it's way."

"What are we going to do?" he wailed.

The smartly-dressed woman sitting opposite the Selfridges' bags turned to the young man next to her.

"Excuse me, can I get out, please? I need to help that girl."

She slid quickly out of her seat, and in a few steps was standing over Maria and Joe.

"It'll be alright, love. My name's Eve, I'm a nurse. Can I have a look at you?"

The businessman in the seat across the aisle lowered his *Financial Times* and stood up, grabbing his briefcase and a carrier bag that clinked as two bottles of festive cheer rubbed together.

"I'll move," he said quickly. "You'll need more room, and privacy."

He pushed past and sat further down the coach.

Eve turned to Maria and said gently, 'Let's have a look, shall we?'

A few moments later she looked up.

"You're right, the baby's on it's way! Let's get you as comfy as we can. We could do with a clean towel and some clean linen but we'll manage.'"

Overhearing her further down the coach a striking young woman, expensively dressed like a fashion model, stood up and lifted her red leather valise down from the luggage rack. Opening it, she drew out a pristine, white hand towel and a bar of soap, and worked her way to the front.

"Will these help? They're unused." She handed them to Eve who smiled with thanks.

The young man who had been sitting next to Eve opened the rucksack at his feet and drew out a white linen shirt still in it's wrapping. He leaned forward into the aisle, holding it out.

"Is this any use?" he asked.

"Are you sure?" Eve queried. "I'll have to tear it."

"It's alright," the young man replied. "I can always buy another!"

"Good lad, son," said his father opposite him, and his mother with the Selfridges' bags smiled at him.

"I've got cold water, but I really could do with some hot," observed Eve, washing her hands in the bottled water Joe had given her.

"I've got a Thermos," called out a woman further down the coach. "I always keep the milk and teabag separately.

They stew if they're left in hot water," she added.

Eve took the Thermos gratefully, tore off the front sleeves of the shirt, and left the back in one piece to wrap the baby in.

"Could I have the unread section of your paper, please?" She called out to the businessman. "Newsprint is pretty sterile. It's the bleaching they use."

Eve gathered everything together and rubbed her hands with antiseptic from a little First Aid kit she kept in her bag.

"Hold her hand Joe, and talk to her. You're going to be alright, love. It's the most natural thing in the world!"

The next 20 minutes were filled with calls and cries and expletives, and the noise of straining; and then suddenly the cry of a baby, and a cheer went up all along the coach.

"It's a little boy!" called out Eve, to another cheer. She cleaned the baby with the torn shirt, and wrapped him in its back, helping Maria place him to her breast, where he nuzzled and suckled urgently.

"We must keep him warm," she said.

The woman behind rummaged in her Selfridges' bags, pulling out a new woollen jumper.

"I got it for him for Christmas," she said, nodding to her husband, "but the baby needs it more!"

There was a rattle beneath them and the train started to move out of the tunnel, to cheers all around.

The man in the seat behind was on his mobile, "Ambulance please, to Orpington Station. Yes, that's right. A woman has just given birth on the train. My name? King. Geoffrey King. No, I'm just a fellow passenger."

The train slid slowly into the station and bright light shone through the window of the coach. Everyone breathed a sigh of relief.

There was wild signalling through the windows. The doors opened, letting in a cold draught of air, and two paramedics carrying a stretcher and blankets. They squeezed along the aisle and soon had the mother and baby snug on a stretcher.

Joe looked around at everyone. "Er, I don't know you, but, well thank you. I don't know what we would have done without you . . . especially . . . " He turned to Eve.

"That's alright, Joe. I've seen many babies into the world, but he will always be special!"

They all looked down on the mother and baby, secure in their shared love. Eve, the Kings, the young model, the businessman in his smart suit, the woman with the Thermos, and all the others, still and silent for a moment. In all of them, a thought was stirring, of the power of a newborn baby to break down barriers between people, and bring out the original goodness of the world.

Brandy Snap
By Jan Steer

She lay in the bottle graveyard, breathing in the acrid, urine-sodden air of the narrow Victorian alleyway behind the pub. She kicked haphazardly at a wet rat that sat investigating her foot with its nose. It squeaked sharply, jumped back in surprise, then scurried down a drain pursued by the woman's slurred obscenities.

Unsteadily, she pulled her aching body together and considered getting to her feet. Her brain, its reasoning power not in the least diminished by the effects of so much cheap brandy, argued against it. She stayed among the decomposing rubbish which occasionally danced in the fetid breeze.

With half-closed eyes, she fought to make sense of her surroundings. Music from the jukebox drifted into the alley, mixed with the shouted oddments of conversation thrown out by the pub's clientele.

Desperate to be a part of the gaiety again, she straightened up. She was still important to the revellers. She loved the sound of the clinking of glasses, the laughter of the drinkers. Nothing else mattered.

But she should sit here for a minute on the cobblestones and recover the remnants of her dignity perhaps. Then she could re-enter to bargain for more alcohol. Perhaps nestle snuggly in the crook of a masculine arm, as a kitten might, and allow a rough hand to stroke at every part of her perspiring flesh. It was all part of a well-practised game, a trade-off. She gave generously and so did the men.

She always said she enjoyed the company of men and liked their smell and texture; their gentleness as their fingers toured her flesh, roaming over her flat places, over the hills and valleys of her breasts. She liked the needle prick of pleasure as they grasped her bottom, squeezing it firmly and pulling her in closer, before pressing their drink-stained lips hard against hers.

That's what men do. Like it or not that is what men do. Best to accept it and enjoy the booze they supply.

She sat in the ooze and tugged at the knees of her stockings, trying to shake them free of the circular water stains which discoloured her shins. She giggled at the impossibility of it and gave up.

She always wore stockings. Men like stockings, most

men anyway. Their searching fingers would seek out the suspender clips hidden under her skirt, roaming over her thighs as they imagined the delights that lay beneath. She could allow that.

Sometimes, she would go into the alley with a special one and let him take her up against the rotting brickwork, or she'd bend herself for him over a sweating metal barrel.

At closing time, she would be poured into a taxi.

When she was younger, a friend might stay the night. Now she no longer cared. She could sleep away the drink alone.

From somewhere up the alley, faint strains of conversation laced with laughter found her. A group of young men, chattering merrily, stared down at her in disbelief. She grinned at them, inanely.

"That's your trouble," one with a refined voice was saying. "You've never got any bloody money." He knelt next to her and lifted her chin with his palm. "Now this is what you need. Some tart, pissed out of her brain, who will come to you willingly – and for free." He let her chin fall and stood up. Her head dropped onto her breast.

"Oh! I see," said his chum. "A sort of strumpet voluntary you mean?" His friend grasped his shoulders with both hands and pointed him down the alley.

"Oh, very funny Charlie boy, mega funny." And they continued making their way over the cobbles, shouting and laughing raucously as they disappeared from view.

She knew she'd been ridiculed and urged herself to fight back in some way. "Piss off you bastards," she mouthed. She could be a lady if she tried.

It was hard to stand. Her head was thumping. She staggered forward and ran into the doorframe. She slithered down it, slightly dazed, and hit the ground. She tried again. With her arm muscles burning now she pulled herself up using a drainpipe for support. She steadied herself against the wall, shook her head and sucked up the rancid air. Then vomited into the gutter. Brandy and bile.

Now feeling hollow, but alive, she began smoothing down the front of her skirt, trying to iron out the wrinkles with her filthy palms, then adjusted her stockings. She pushed open the pub door. The familiar hot and stale breath of the room swam into her nose and she stepped confidently back into the dance, that grotesque polka, the one that she had for so long now made her own. The rebellious throng widened its arms, offered up its soul, opened its foul mouth – and swallowed her whole.

That Was the Year
By Audrey Yeardley

That was the year I went a bit crazy. Just a bit – more outraged really, but enough to scare myself.

"And quite right too," said My Self. "You shouldn't have allowed that."

For a while, everything transformed itself into something like an ancient Greek play by Euripides (and me playing Clytemnestra, with her Not So's!) what with one thing and another. Those Old Ones knew a lot about Emotions, if you ask me. And what follows, when we mess with them.

When a man lies, it hurts.

It changes you.

I speak personally, of course.

Some women cut their hair, change the colours, go spiky, have tattoos scratched into their shoulders, get into black leather and high-heeled boots. Go feral.

That is what I did, for a whole year.

Andre said I wasn't to waste any more time grieving; that it was his loss and not mine; that any man who'd work on someone's emotions like that wasn't worth a penny; and I should get myself to Egypt.

He was right about the first bits; got the directions wrong for the last. But yes, when you're dealing with Old Stuff, that's where you have to go seeking: in the Long Time Ago Stuff, seeking the clues.

I went back to my books. The ones I'd been poring over since I'd first had the dreams; the ones I'd taught myself to read so that I could retrieve the necessary information for some of what had been, and what might be coming.

I might have gone a little bit crazy with my emotions but intellectually, I was up to speed.

Tragedy: a protagonist falls to disaster through personal folly and circumstances they cannot control.

"Ha!" I say to My Self. "Told you."

When I look back, as I do now, there had been plenty of warnings.

The woman turning up the cards, looking askance at the layout: "You've put yourself on a very high road and there's a grave danger of falling over." Looking at me in an almost-scared way, as in, "Rather you than me."

The Gypsy woman crossing the road to tell me (in an exasperated way), "You've gone and don't it again, haven't you!" And another crossing a busy street in London, refusing to take any money for the bunch of heather she'd pressed into my hand, saying, "Take care, my dear."

There'd been more than enough signals for me (My Self) alone to have worked out that all was not as it seemed; that I was looking through a glass darkly.

That wardrobe you'd claimed as your own with all its empty clothes hangers. The burnt remains of all those business letters you'd accumulated in the old dustbin hidden behind the shed.

It wasn't as though I hadn't taken note. It wasn't until afterwards that I'd really understood why you brought a dog with you in the cluttered van on that last visit (so that there was no room for me to go back with you). And that I knew who you'd been phoning when you went into the garden.

I chose not to take heed. Thinking you'd never mess with a goddess.

You had.

Not now, you wouldn't. Not the Me with my bright red hair, black leather trousers and high-heeled boots, holding the grief, the rage and the pain. Seeking answers. Observing the men observing the women, in the ways you had observed me; making their moves, in those same old ways.

Not after the call you made, at noon. Telling me it

wasn't convenient for me to come up to meet you. You had a new lady friend – nothing serious (it wouldn't make any difference to our friendship) – but it wouldn't be right.

That's what you said.

And I'm remembering your answer, when I'd asked, "What is she like?"

"Oh, Tiddles. She's just an ordinary woman."

And then the silence.

I remember that silence – and how it felt.

Outrage: a gross offence to moral feelings; wanton mischief; a violation: rape.

They say there are seven gates at the entrance to the Underworld – where some are brought low and naked to humility. Stripped bare of all pretensions to the point of destruction and transformation and left to the Will of the Fates.

Some say it was so for Persephone, when she went seeking poppies for her mother.

Some say the gates are opened for us by an unconscious request to discover who we truly are.

It is a heavy price to pay.

There would come a time when I would put my hand on the Rowan Tree, ripening in my powers to curse you. I would listen, then, to My Self, saying, "What goes around, comes around."

There would come a time when a dog walked with

me to the water's edge, where I would watch every torn letter float away into the sea. And the dog, putting its paw on my knee, would gaze at me for a long time, waiting for my tears to dry.

There would come a time when strangers would perform random acts of kindness: and I'd feel gratitude.

And there would come a time when you no longer mattered.

. . .

On the first day I had come to this place where I hoped to find Truth, I had discovered a labyrinth with a deep pit at its centre. I had walked round and around (like a teddy bear, one step, two steps) until I reached the centre; and more steps down to its depths. It had seemed very dark but now there was enough light inside to make out narrow benches along the lengths of each wall.

I sat in this earthy twilight, feeling safe and saving the sensation for when I didn't. It gave me a strange kind of comfort: this was a place where I could come (in the afterwards) when I had travelled through an even darker place and been unravelled.

And then I set about cutting my hair (as some do, from grief) and colouring it, and began to wear black leather and high boots; and went to the place where Truth is sought.

. . .

On the last evening we'd all come together in a large

hall transformed with plants lit by candles. Silver river with a bridge divided the men and the women. All day we had sat, separately, speaking honestly with each other; celebrating how far we had come.

We had simply looked at each other for a while.

The men looked so good and wholesome, and they were happy. A distant voice said we were welcome to go to the bridge to speak from our hearts; to ask a question; to express something had been hidden for too long.

For a while we looked at each other.

A man got up, walked to the bridge to say his piece. Another followed, then another, until a woman got up to speak her truth.

And I knew it was time to speak mine, shaking from being silent for too long (even though the man, who should have been listening, was not here), walking to the bridge, and said it anyway.

They had listened.

For a very brief moment, the men across the silver river had the semblance of gods; then they became men again.

And I, with my coloured hair, black leather trousers and high boots, became less of a goddess. More of a woman.

The House in Montmartre
By Peter Lewis

The house in Montmartre, in the shadow of the Sacre Coeur, was old. Other houses in the street had an air of neglect but mine had been cared for. I say mine because it is now my house.

I'd become friendly with Madame Jospin when I helped her home one day after she'd fallen in the street. I did odd jobs for her and kept her company during the day. At night I worked as a sous chef in a restaurant near Pigalle.

She made me laugh at the stories she told, in her throaty voice with echoes of her former sensuality, chain-smoking, sipping cognac and cursing.

She would often chide me for coming onto the scene too late for her to seduce me.

When she died, I was the only mourner at her funeral. Shortly afterwards I was invited to the notaire's office to be told I had been left the house in her will.

I gave up my dingy flat as soon as I had the keys to my new abode and, with my meagre belongings in two holdalls, I unlocked the front door and walked in to the place I'd come to love. Of course, it was no longer the same. I could still smell the Gauloises, though, and I almost expected Madame to appear, grumbling, at any moment.

The house had three stories; on the ground floor there was an unused kitchen at one end with a dumb waiter from where food would have been taken to the second floor. Carpeted stairs led up to this floor. There were five rooms: a large, well-furnished sitting room, a kitchen-dining room, two bedrooms and a bathroom. Madame's was to be my bedroom. Up more stairs were another three rooms, the original servants' quarters, I presumed.

On my first night, I prepared my speciality, a cassoulet, which I ate in the dining room, pretending I was Monsieur, the wealthy owner of the house; a bottle of St Emilion '85 went down a treat and I enjoyed a selection of cheeses. A brandy followed and I fell asleep within seconds of getting into bed. That's when it started.

I woke suddenly and couldn't get my bearings; the room was in darkness. I hadn't slept well and I felt as if something had woken me. I lay listening to the sounds of the house. It sighed, creaked, complained, rather like Madame Jospin, I thought. I turned on the light to see the time and glimpsed a ball of smoke roll off my bed, across the floor and under the door. I kept the light on after that and eventually slept.

When a little light came into the room, I lay thinking about what had happened and decided I'd imagined it. Last night's cheese was the culprit. After all, here I was, unharmed. I opened the curtains and watched Paris stirring on a fresh April morning; a milk cart rattled down the street, gutters were running to wash away the night's rubbish, passers-by on their way to work, the blind beggar who sat outside the entrance to the *Place du Tertre*, an artist on her way to the Place.

I was working that night and I spent the day examining Madame's possessions, deciding what to keep and what I'd sell. There was a flea-market nearby where I would get a good price for some of them. I wasn't being mercenary; I intended to buy a headstone for her grave.

After my shift, I turned in early, deciding to keep a light on, not because I was afraid but because I felt I would sleep better. I didn't. I woke sweating from a nightmare; a weight was pinning me down and I couldn't breathe. I tried to push away whatever was on top of me but my arms wouldn't respond. Just as I felt I would die from lack of air I woke up. Apart from a dishevelled bed, nothing seemed wrong.

I still didn't feel scared, slept again and woke feeling

refreshed. As I lay contemplating what I would do that day, I heard a strange noise. A clock was ticking. There was an ancient grandfather downstairs but it hadn't worked for years, Madame had told me. When it gave up the ghost, she didn't have it repaired because she said the ticking reminded her of her life ebbing away.

I ran downstairs and saw the old clock was definitely working. It didn't show the right time but it ticked as confidently as when it was made. Up to that point nothing had happened to make me feel uneasy. But who had wound up the clock? I stared at it as if it would give me the answer but it just stared nonchalantly back.

Nothing out of the ordinary happened for a few days and on the Saturday I'd invited friends, Jacques and Antoine, for dinner. At the cheese course, the air suddenly turned exceptionally cold. We all noticed it and looked at the door to see if it had opened. It hadn't.

Then the light flickered once and died. There were lit candles on the dining table and, moving to the window, I saw that Montmartre was blacked out. Jacques was unsettled.

"It shouldn't be this cold, Matthieu. Is there a door open?"

We left the table and went downstairs to the front door. Bolted. Then Antoine shouted in alarm, "Look! The cellar door's open. That's where the cold is coming from."

I'd been in the cellar occasionally when Madame was

alive but I hadn't been down since I moved into the house. We crept down the steps. I was wondering if someone was playing tricks on me. Someone who didn't want me in the house. We saw nothing unusual but felt an unnatural iciness in the air.

"There's something I don't like here," whispered Jacques.

"He's right. It shouldn't be this cold," said Antoine, "but there's obviously nothing here. Let's go and finish our meal. Perhaps we haven't drunk enough of Matthieu's excellent wine. Bring another bottle up, *mon ami*."

We returned to the table and talked quietly. The lights flickered on and made us jump and laugh. The air became warm again.

"Have you got a resident ghost, *mon ami*?"

"I don't believe in ghosts or hauntings, Antoine," replied Jacques. "When one is dead that's that. Life is miserable enough without anyone wanting more of if. No, when you are underground you stay there."

"Ever the existentialist, Jacques," I laughed. "But what about people who die and are not buried? Couldn't there be unquiet spirits seeking a resting place?"

"Why would they cause trouble or scare people?"

"Do you believe there is evil in the world?" I said. "I'm thinking of Nazis, Stalin. Child-molesters . . ."

"I believe there is a spirit of evil," said Jacques, "That some people tap into through choice or accident."

"And if that is the case does the evil die with the person who had committed evil deeds?"

Suddenly, we became aware of an odour. A rancid stench that was like no other I'd ever experienced. Jacques began to gag and I rushed to open a window. The smell disappeared as quickly as it had come and Antoine joked that, as it was my house, I could behave how I liked in it.

At that moment, our eyes were drawn to the dumb waiter. It had rattled into operation. Jacques was over to it in a second. He caught the full blast of whatever emanated from the hatch and collapsed on the spot. Dead.

Antoine and I half-stood at the table, unable to comprehend what we were seeing. Something inexplicably grotesque writhed slowly in and out of the dumb waiter. Antoine shrieked and stumbled from the room cursing. I heard the front door open and he was gone.

I'm told that my mind, unable to accept what I'd seen, has simply shut down. I was found next morning, still at the table, gibbering uncontrollably.

I sit here now, looking over the grounds, calm as long as I take my medication. I will never return to Madame's house. Someone else is welcome to it. Antoine took his own life; I read of his death in the newspaper.

The sun shines agreeably in through the open window. I can hear birdsong and the pleasant rustle of the trees. I am content.

Thursday's Shepherd's Pie
By Mandy Fouracre

A mid-grey wash of cloud hung low over the garden. Seven coloured pegs clung to the rotating washing line. One for every day of the week. *Monday's washing day.* The lyric leapt out of Sarah's memory and she sang it silently, absentmindedly as she gazed out of the window into the murky evening sky.

Tuesday's soup. Wednesday's roast beef, Thursday's shepherd's pie.

Today was Thursday and, in accord with the rhyme, shepherd's pie was in the oven. Shepherd's pie prepared as instructed.

Sarah's gaze quickly flicked around the room. Everything clean, surfaces wiped, no clutter, coats hung in the cupboard, outdoor shoes on the shoe rack, children's toys in the box.

In the kitchen were carrots cut in uniform sticks, not

circles, broccoli florets in equal sizes, parsley ready to be chopped on the chopping board. The steamer ready on the hob, kettle boiled and olive oil ready to be drizzled. Table laid.

The children sat at one end of the table, their heads almost touching as they leant over their colouring and sticking books. Their hair shone golden and silky under the pendant lamp.

Beautiful, healthy, innocent. Perfect. Love for them, in a dart, pierced her heart.

She glanced at the timer on the oven. Her mouth felt dry. She poured a glass of filtered water and drank, unconsciously wiping the spout of the chrome water filter until it shone, reflecting a distorted image of her face.

Fly me to the moon was playing quietly on the radio in the background as she washed and dried the glass.

At the end of the song a timecheck was given by the presenter in a fun, chatty, ordinary way. It was 5.30pm. Thousands of people in the kitchens of homes around the country would be hearing the same timecheck.

It chimed exactly with the sound of the key in the front door, followed by the door opening and closing. The keys were thrown into the wooden bowl on the narrow window sill to the left of the front door.

Sarah knew then, simply by practised listening, that he was not in a good mood.

Today it was Mr Nasty who had arrived home although it was Mr Nice she had met and dated and married.

Mr Nice, through constant endeavour, gained an exemplary status in the workplace and amongst his work colleagues. At home Mr Nasty was Mr Nice stripped bare.

The children looked up from their colouring books.

"Is daddy home, mummy?" they asked in unison. Sarah nodded and suggested that they wait for him to shower and change before going in to the sitting room to say hello.

On days like today, the safest strategy was to keep out of the way until he decided to join them.

About 15 minutes later he came into the kitchen and took a cold beer from the fridge, checking and rechecking the bottle with his hand to ensure that it was the correct temperature.

He looked across at the children and said, "Hello kids."

They ran over on cue and hugged him in a well-controlled display of practised affection. They had learned to please him.

As he took his beer into the sitting room Sarah said that dinner would be about 15 minutes if that suited.

"I'll let you know when I'm ready to eat," he replied and as he closed the door he shouted that she should turn the radio down.

Sarah stared at the radio. It was barely audible even to

her and she was standing less than two feet away from it. The doors were closed, it couldn't possibly disturb him. She didn't turn it down.

The voice of the cheerful radio presenter provided a tenuous link to an ordinary everyday-ness which other people were experiencing in their homes. The normality was comforting.

"I thought I said to turn that radio down," he shouted three minutes later.

Sarah resignedly leant towards the radio with an unsteady hand. Her fingers slipped on the volume control – she had turned the volume up instead of down.

Sarah froze and waited. Mouth dry again, her body emptied of all energy.

His footsteps were the first indication of the degree of his anger. The stamping weight of his 13 stone body in every step. That, and the way he slammed the sitting room door. The children looked at Sarah and then at the door. Struck mute.

They had all taken their positions in a bizarre family tableau.

He burst into the kitchen, turned the radio off and stood in front of Sarah, facing her squarely. His eyes were shining with venomous hatred.

He pointed his finger directly towards her face almost touching her nose.

"You bitch. You fucking ugly bitch. Don't you appreciate the fact that I've been working all day. When I come home I want quiet, QUIET! Do you hear me?" he shouted.

Sarah knew he wasn't going to stop there. This was just the beginning. She waited.

"I don't know why I married you. You fat, ugly bitch. Look at you – so bloody ugly. I'm ashamed of you. What a fool I was to marry you, you ugly fat bitch."

He grabbed hold of her hair and pulled her face towards the wooden mirror on the wall which had two hearts on either side. He twisted her head round so that she could see her reflection.

"Look at that ugly mug. That's you, my wife, and I'm stuck with you. STUCK WITH YOU – you fucking bitch."

He pulled her body upright by her hair and flung her away. She landed against the cooker. He walked across slowly like a boxer coming out of his corner for Round 2. *Seconds away.*

Standing facing her again, bending down, he spat out, "Why don't you just take yourself off and go and die somewhere? That would be the best thing you could do for everyone. Yep – go and die somewhere, you hateful ugly bitch."

He grabbed her ears and shook her, "I've thought

over and over again so many times how to get rid of you, bitch."

He flung her this time against the work surface. The chopping board on which the carrots and broccoli were so perfectly prepared, bounced, as did the oil.

Her hand fumbled behind her back trying to grab on to something to steady herself. The chopping board tumbled onto the floor.

The immaculately clean floor became a serving platter for the vegetable medley. Olive oil streaked visibly and invisibly making its own quiet, meandering, liquid pattern.

Sarah braced herself for Round 3. *Seconds away.*

"You stupid fucking ugly bitch; nobody else would want you," he yelled, rushing at her, stopping only to pick up the steamer which he raised above her head.

He paused, allowing himself to luxuriate in the power of the moment.

The children screamed, "Daddy, NO!"

It sounded as though they were in an echo chamber because the NO went on and on.

He turned his body towards them and as he did so he slipped on the olive oil.

Time slowed at that point. His arms clutched at the air in a desperate attempt to right his balance. His feet slithered and slipped, he looked surprised at the turn of events. He fell to the floor as if in slow motion.

The awkwardness of falling in such a small space meant that there was not enough room for the whole of his body. His head hit the corner of the cooker on the way down and again as he landed. It was an awkward landing. He lay motionless, part of the steamer still in his hand.

The children ran towards her. They all hugged. And hugged again more tightly. And then they cried in a collective release of suspended fear and tension.

Sarah crept nearer to him. She couldn't see his chest rising and falling. She couldn't hear his breath inhaling or exhaling.

He was quiet and very, very still, almost peaceful.

The atmosphere was still and peaceful.

Sarah asked the children to fetch her phone from the kitchen table and she rang 999.

Bartlett, the Dog and the Old Sailor
By Ron Hardwick

It is a beautiful morning. The sun is shining, birds are bursting their lungs and everything in the garden is growing like mad. It is a day for activity, exploration, and aesthetic pleasure from the landscape. In short, it is a day for doing something.

Bartlett, with his little black spaniel, drives down to his favourite spot by the sea, some 20 miles from his modest terraced house. He's been there before. It is a tiny hamlet perched high on clifftops, looking out over the vast expanse of ocean. It feels like, any day now, the houses could simply slide a hundred feet down the cliffs and into the sea.

There's a car park for a dozen cars and a vertiginous path leading to the bay. This is reached by way of an uneven and pitch-dark tunnel hewn through the cliffs. For a claustrophobic like Bartlett, walking through it is an unnerving experience, although there is the comfort of a pin-prick of light at the far end. In such places he tends to recall the time he was stuck in a lift on a red-hot summer's day, with 20 other people who thought they were about to meet their maker – until Bartlett prised open the lift doors by sheer brute force and the crowd fell out into the foyer.

Bartlett and the dog pass through the tunnel into the sunlight and find themselves in an exquisite little bay, bounded by ancient rocks. A man once told him the rocks are four hundred million years old, from what he calls the Silurian period, but Bartlett is sceptical. How can anyone know?

On one side of the bay, there is a manmade harbour of stone where an old sailor is busily working on his boat. Apart from him, and a woman lounging in a nearby garden, there is no-one else around.

The old sailor's hair is snow-white under his jaunty cap. He looks like Captain Birdseye. He is bending low in the fo'c'sle of his boat. He holds a screwdriver and a spanner in one hand and a hammer in the other. By the state of his craft, it appears that these are the only tools he is likely to need. It looks like a Morris Cowley engine, Bartlett thought, circa 1926. Everyone knows how basic these are and how simple they are to work on.

Beyond the harbour wall, there is not a single craft on

the vast expanse of ocean, which, as far as the eye can see, is dead calm. The sun shines on the shimmering water, refracting the light into a million pixels of colour. Bartlett and the dog climb the dozen or so steps cut into the harbour wall and walk past a score of lobster-pots piled high on the narrow pathway. There is a drop of fifteen feet to the water. Suddenly, breaking the silence, the old sailor hails him.

"Can you do me a favour?"

"If I can."

"Are my keys in the van?"

An ancient pick-up truck stands at the foot of the road leading back to the hamlet. It has once been black, but is now mainly rust-coloured. The keys are in the door.

"The keys are in the door," says Bartlett.

"Can you throw them down, please?" asks the old sailor.

Bartlett looks at the distance between the old sailor and him, and remembers that he could never hit a set of cricket stumps from more than three feet away, let alone drop keys into the prow of a boat 15 feet below with a lot of deep sea around it. The old sailor doesn't look as though he owns a spare set.

"I think not," says Bartlett.

"What's to be done, then?" asks the old sailor.

"I'll tell you what I'll do, I'll hide them under the

driver's seat. They can stay there until you're ready to come back up. No-one will find them."

Bartlett cannot imagine for one second anyone wanting to steal that old rust-bucket, but he opens the door, moves aside three empty tins of Tam O'Shanter pipe tobacco and an old fish-and-chip wrapper, and duly hides the keys.

"That's it done."

"Fine. Thank you. Saves me coming up just yet."

"You a fisherman?" asks Bartlett, without curiosity.

The dog sits obediently by his side, displaying only a few signs of boredom. Overhead a few arctic terns screech messages to each other before plummeting into the sea like tiny black and white skyrockets returning to earth.

"Used to be. Retired now," says the old sailor.

"You used to fish round here?"

"Out there." The old sailor gestures vaguely in the direction of the sea.

"A hard life," reflects Bartlett.

"Yep. Worse in winter. Fine, on days like this. Still, the seas were teeming with fish in them days. Not so now."

"European directives?"

"Spaniards. Hoovered up the fish in their huge factory ships until there was hardly any left. They were tough times, they were. Pleased I'm finished with that game."

"You live round here?"

The old sailor points at the clifftop. "Up there. Seaview Cottage. You'll see it on your way back up. Can't miss it. Couple of ribs off of a whale at the front gate."

"A whale?"

"Washed up. Twenty years ago. A minke. Got lost. Ended up in shallow water in the harbour. Compass all wrong. Folk came from miles around to see it. They'd never seen one before. Not a massive creature, not like them humpbacks. Lovely, they is. Delicate, really. More like a shark than a whale. Cigar-shaped. Leap like dolphins, clean out of the water. Clever creatures, whales. Talk to each other. Often wondered how they grew so huge living on tiny plankton."

"Something in their metabolism, no doubt," says Bartlett, who knows nothing about the metabolism of whales. You don't get the chance to see many whales when you're working in an office.

The old sailor shrugs his shoulders.

"How long have you had her?" asks Bartlett.

"The wife?"

"The boat."

"Well, let me see now. Callaghan was prime minister. It was the winter of discontent. I was discontented then, I can tell you. No fish, you see. Ted Ford went bankrupt. I got the boat for a song. She's an old girl."

"Ancient," says Bartlett. "What's she called?"

"Mary-Anne, after the wife. That's her name, see."

There is something poignant in the way the old sailor says this, Bartlett notices. He wonders if the wife is ill, or worse.

The dog tugs at his trouser-cuffs. She is becoming restless, and hungry.

"Nice to talk to you," says Bartlett. "Must go now. Dog's fretting."

The old sailor waves his spanner in lieu of a verbal response.

Bartlett and the dog climb the steep path to the hamlet. Whatever the old sailor does with his hammer, screwdriver and spanner must work, for ten minutes later, as the pair finally reach the hamlet, Bartlett sees the old sailor's boat chugging out of the harbour and into the wide blue ocean. It looks like a fly in a swimming-pool.

"Sooner him than me," Bartlett says to the dog. He wonders what might become of the old sailor if his ancient engine stops wheezing and he is cast adrift, becalmed, left to the mercy of unpredictable tides.

He soon sees that the old sailor has the same thoughts himself, as he promptly turns the boat round and heads back to the safety of the harbour. He has sailed a matter of three hundred yards. Bartlett laughs.

He has scarcely seen any views so remarkable. He observes Seaview Cottage with its whalebones at the gate. There is beetroot maturing in the front garden. The windows need a lick of paint. The old sailor's wife is hanging out washing. Her aged skin is cracked as dried seaweed. She doesn't look ill, or worse, just old.

Bartlett learns from a plaque at the end of the single street that the hamlet was once a tidy little herring port. The sheltered harbour must have been a magnet for smugglers. At its peak, the place housed over fifty people; not all of them were smugglers. He also discovers that eleven fishermen died on the night of the great storm of 1889. They all met their end in full view of their families standing watching from the shore.

He drives home past the bloodied remains of a red deer that an inconsiderate lorry has slaughtered in the early hours of the morning. A motorway sign reads *Deer on the Road*. Bartlett guesses the lorry-driver didn't read it.

Our Aftermath
By Marion Horton

Metal curtain hooks screeched across the rails. Like a braking train. I shouted, "Rob, Rob. Just look at this!" You tried to shush me. You shuffled your body over the bed and dragged yourself up, leaning your arm on my shoulder.

And then you saw.

A mass of shiny, wet leaves was pressed up against the window pane. The nearest tree should have been 20 feet away and now it was leaning against our house.

You flicked on the light switch. Nothing happened so you flicked it three, four more times. Nothing. You swore. You were never a morning person.

We fumbled in the half-light to find our clothes then you went ahead of me down the stairs. I took each step slowly, one hand on the bannister, one on my stomach. *Watch it, Moira. The fall down the stairs the week before . . .*

I didn't need reminding. You still hadn't fixed the loose stair rod.

The ground floor of the house was dark, cave-like. I opened the curtains in the lounge and crushed up against the window was a nest hanging from a branch. It stared back at me. Like a monster's eye hanging by a sinew.

You went into the kitchen and I heard the radio. Madonna was playing. Then came the opening beeps of the 8 o'clock news. You called for me to come and listen, "Gusts of over 100 miles per hour have hit the South East, leaving devastation in their wake . . ."

We stepped outside. No traffic, no birds. Is it possible to hear a silence?

Our neighbours stood in the road. All stunned. Trees were felled, fences smashed, gates crumpled, gardens pummelled. Our leafy road was ripped up. And all the sky open above us, there was an ocean of it. We craned our necks up to take it in.

You said it was crazy. Then you ran up the road to look at more devastation.

A neighbour commented on the kids playing. I don't think she meant you. Children were swarming over the fallen trunks, splashing in the puddles of muddy water, fighting with broken branches.

One chestnut tree had left behind a crater the size of a paddling pool. A little girl with tiny red wellington boots was splashing in its centre. Roots as thick as my wrist dripped from the fallen tree. Some stretched from the torn-up base into the wet mud like a giant cat's cradle.

What could we do? The fire brigade? We shook our heads. No, we wouldn't be a priority. People mumbled and fretted. Then you came back with our neighbour Reg.

The pair of you were toting chainsaws. You had goggles on. That surprised me, until I realised they were probably for effect – part of the look. I saw an excited grin on your face as you yanked on the cord of your chainsaw. Reg put his goggles on too. He raised his chainsaw up in the air as it leapt into life. A pair of wartime fighter pilots ready for battle. You were impatient to get started. You headed for the chestnut tree. Rob and Reg. Our heroes. Here to save the day.

The noise from the chainsaws was deafening and petrol fumes filled the air. I walked away to talk to another neighbour. We watched you both with your heads down, mouths set, chunks of wood flying in the air. You were having a great time slicing through that massive trunk of ancient wood.

No work and no school. The change of routine felt liberating. For a while.

You and Reg had sawed for quite some time. And then it came. A crack to split the ears lashed through the air. The ground shook with such a thud I felt it deep inside my body, beneath my stretched coat.

The chestnut's trunk had been completely sliced through. The half that was still held on by the giant roots had snapped back into the crater, like a monster's tooth being sucked back into its socket.

Brown water and wet soil gobbed out. There was a hush – it was thick and heavy. No-one spoke. We just looked at the grass verge next to where the trunk had snapped back into its hole. Lying on the grass was a muddied red wellington boot.

You both smiled and nodded. Ignorant and blissful. Mission accomplished. But the rest of us looked at the place where the little girl in the red wellington boots had been happily splashing. A slice of trunk ten feet high stood firmly back in the ground. The crater had gone. And so had she.

Someone moaned. I felt sick.

How long did we stand there, frozen, impotent? I don't know. At some point the child's mother called out her name. She saw the red boot. *Where was her child? What were we staring at?* Someone pointed towards the base of the tree. I think their hand was shaking.

The mother walked up to the tree and looked at us the way you looked at me when I told you about the baby. *What do you mean? Stop mucking about.*

You took your goggles off then. Confused that there

was no applause perhaps. We watched as the mother bent to pick up the dripping boot. A cloud of wood dust fell gently like ash onto our heads and shoulders. I thought of Pompeii for some reason. The mother held up the boot, examining it like an exhibit from one of those crime programmes you like so much. A child's squeal broke her concentration. She turned towards the sound and marched off waving the boot, shouting out her daughter's name.

I don't think anyone told the mother what we thought had happened. I felt a guilt I thought we all felt – until I heard your reaction. You said you didn't know what all the fuss was about. *No-one was hurt, were they? For Christ's sake Moira, lighten up.* I believe you still wanted a pat on the back for sawing up the chestnut tree.

You rested your hand on my stomach later that evening to feel the tiny feet kicking.

I couldn't ignore what had happened. I had seen you in a different light. And things would have to change. I moved your hand away.

"Rob."

You looked at me. Did you hear a different tone in my voice?

"We have to talk."

Father Christmas
By David Stephens

We're both instantly recognisable. Me in my ill-fitting red suit, stick-on white beard, bag of Christmas presents; he with my wife's pale blue eyes, his long thin fingers, and that endearing expression of permanent curiosity that I think he inherited from his grandmother. Perhaps, if I'd given the job more thought, I'd have considered the outside chance he'd visit. He's of that age now and was always one for the mystery and fantasy of Christmas.

He enters the grotto like most children, tentative but with a heightened sense of expectation. Health and Safety now insist that each visitor no longer perches on Santa's lap but sits opposite on a specially provided red plastic chair decorated for the occasion with a layer of fake snow and tinsel. He stands politely in front of me waiting to be told he can sit.

Keep to the script. Listen to the child's wishes. Avoid

answering any questions about religion or politics and of course avoid all physical contact. Ask what they want in their stocking or under the tree, engage them in two or three minutes of harmless conversation, give them the parting gift, and then wave them goodbye. Clear?

Couldn't be clearer.

And remember each visit to the grotto is to last for no more than four minutes.

He sits down and folds his hands politely in his lap. He leans forward and looks closely at my beard and glasses. I am what he expects to see. Nothing more.

Allow the child to ask the first question.

He does.

"Where do you live?"

A legitimate question on script.

"Well, I live in the far North, young man, where the cold winds blow and the reindeer are ready and waiting to pull my sleigh full of wonderful presents for every good little boy and girl."

Actually I live, if you can call it a living, not far from Salford in a grotty tower block along with a bunch of transient students occasionally taken to feeling sorry for the lonely old git upstairs . . .

He seems satisfied with my answer. I ask him what he wants for Christmas. While he considers the answer, I take the opportunity to have a good look at him. He's changed a lot in two years. Taller, more robust, a slightly deeper pitch to his voice, his face showing signs of a fall or scratch.

Why wasn't I there to pick him up, repair the skateboard, commiserate? I'll tell you why. Because I'm the selfish bastard who took the easy way out, only to find there was no easy way back. And now there's no going back. Never. She's made sure of that.

"So, what would you like for Christmas?" He looks surprised but sits down on the red plastic chair with its fake snow.

"I'd like some paints and some drawing paper and a box for keeping all the stuff in."

"That's quite a list. And what will you paint?"

Neither of us had any interest or talent in art, but perhaps he's been inspired at school or from a friend? Or her new friend. Believe me, she'll have a new friend.

He pauses for longer this time, perhaps surprised I should be so interested.

"A picture of my new house and the park next door for my daddy to see. He's never seen it. Not my new daddy, he's called Alan, but my real daddy who's not here anymore and hasn't seen the house and the park and the lamp post where I lock my bike in case it gets stolen."

Keep to the script. No physical contact of any kind. Just talk, hand over the present, and wave them goodbye . . .

Wave them goodbye. I am good at that. I've got form.

Standing in the drive, waiting to leave but not wanting to go. Noticing that the front hedge needed a good trim. She, tight-lipped and furious, and my son looking up at me with those pale blue eyes, saying nothing, but aware that something was wrong. This time he'd sensed things were different. This time Daddy might be going away and not coming back.

She stood there in her bright red duffel coat – it suited her – a protective arm around his waist, saying nothing as I reversed the car out of the drive and left. Looking back, I saw him return my wave, his right-hand half-raised, his long thin fingers tucked inside the red and white gloves I'd left in his stocking on Christmas Eve.

'From Father Christmas, to keep your hands warm', I'd written on the note by the bed. Crap father, but not a bad Santa.

"You're going to paint a picture for your daddy?" I asked.

"With the paints and paper, you give me from your sack."

I reach into the sack and take out a small wrapped parcel. As far as I can remember the small gifts contain wax crayons, a small tube of glitter and some child-proof adhesive, but no paper.

He puts the small parcel inside his pocket.

"Ask your mum or your dad to give you some paper."

He stands up to leave.

"Wait a minute, lad, I have something else."

His pale blue eyes watch me reach inside my tunic. I

take out the five-pound note I'd saved for my lunch and hand it to him. He looks at it for a moment and then puts it carefully into his trouser pocket.

"And how will you give your real daddy the painting? Of your house and the park . . . "

He thinks for a moment and then smiles, pleased with himself.

"I won't. I don't know where he lives, and Mummy won't tell me. But I have a plan."

"A plan?"

"I can give it to you, and when you get to his house on Christmas Eve you can go down his chimney and leave it next to his bed!"

On no account must you show any emotion in front of any child, even if they get over-excited or upset. If the latter occurs take the child by the hand and walk the child to the awaiting parent or supervising adult outside.

"You know you'll have to come back here to give it to me, don't you?"

He smiles again, clearly expecting the question.

"Alan said that I can have anything I want this Christmas, so I'll tell him that I want to come back here and see you so I can give you my painting. Okay?"

I tell him it's more than okay, a master plan and one that wouldn't fail.

He moves towards the entrance. A polite child, he

holds out his right hand, our long thin fingers touching briefly. He looks up and says nothing, his pale blue eyes taking in my white stick-on beard and ill-fitting red suit.

When they leave wish them a Happy Christmas.

"And a happy Christmas young man to you and your family. I shall be thinking of you."

He turns to leave, and then stops for a moment.

"Can I tell you something else?"

I nod, wondering what he's going to say.

I wait.

"I don't like my new daddy. He's mean. He says I can have anything I want, but he sometimes changes his mind."

I move closer towards him and smile as best as I can.

"It's not easy having a new daddy. But I'm sure he loves you."

"As much as you love me?"

"Yes, as much as I love you. And as much as your mummy loves you."

"And as much as my real daddy loves me?"

"Yes, as much as he does too."

Outside I can hear the mumbled voices of a parent waiting for her child to be invited in.

"Till tomorrow, then."

"Till tomorrow."

I touch his hand once more.

And then he's gone.

Vulnerable
By Annette Byford

She had not expected that. Which was a ridiculous thing to think, as if anybody had been able to predict it. We all seemed to be at the centre of a science fiction film, waking up in the morning wondering whether this was really happening.

But it was happening. She stood at the window and for a long time looked out on the familiar emptiness of her street. No traffic, only the odd jogger running past. Sometimes it was parents now running together with their children, a good idea clearly and they tended to look quite pleased with themselves. You could tell the ones who had never done any of this before, looking puffed and slightly awkward, in contrast to the experienced runners with their special gear in garish colours, slightly put out by all these newcomers.

Dog walkers following their daily routine as if nothing

had changed, the odd couple striding out purposefully. Everyone circling around each other, with a mixture of awkwardness, anxiety and irritation, glad to be out, equally glad to scuttle back into the safety of their homes. Mostly though the street was eerily empty and there was nobody to be seen at all.

What she had not expected was how her own life would change, the strange details of it all. She stared at her phone screen where the WhatsApp messages from her book group members were beginning to pop up. This would go on now, all day long. Barred from seeing each other, from seeing anyone in fact, seemed to have unleashed wave after wave of connecting virtually.

It had been such a boost in the early days, to know that you were not on your own, that there were people out there who cared about you and who were part of your social and emotional network. Staying in touch through video calls and via messages and sharing photos had made all the difference.

Ping, another message. Nicola apparently had made more progress with her garden and her seedlings were doing well. More pings, and other group members were sending photos of their gardens. Wasn't it wonderful, all the birdsong, and wasn't the sky so much clearer now with less pollution, and had the pace of life not changed for the better. Erica had posted photos of her repainted garden furniture and the new tabletop, decorated with pieces of coloured glass which she had collected at the beach. The table sparkled in the sun, as did the glass of wine, lifted to say cheers, Erica with a beaming smile.

She hesitated, thinking about how to respond and wiped the worktops in the kitchen, again. What was mostly on her mind was the Zoom conversation she had had with her adult children over the weekend. The children now rang quite frequently and the weekend Zoom call, often combined with a family quiz, had become a regular feature of their week.

She was touched by the fact that both her daughter and her son were clearly making an effort to stay in touch. She would not have taken that for granted after years of doing all the running, after years of wondering how long this one-way traffic of attention and effort between mother and adult child would continue.

Something seemed to have shifted. As if the repeated talk of older people being more vulnerable had changed something in her children's perception of her. From being the invincible matriarch of unlimited resources, who could be called upon whenever there was a crisis, she seemed to have morphed within a month into an older person who was vulnerable. This was a new experience. Quite how she felt about it, she was not sure.

During the Zoom conversation yesterday she had told

her children how much she was looking forward to the hairdresser opening again and having her roots done and a good cut. Her son had been quite forceful: what was she thinking of? Given her age, was a haircut really so important to take such a risk, with the virus still out there and, again, at her age? She could, with some effort, with some considerable effort, remind herself, that this comment came from a place of concern and wanting to see her safe.

More WhatsApp messages. It was exercise time in book group land. Monica had discovered online Zumba, Moya had taken up running with the *From Couch to 5k* app, all of them were jokingly contrasting their fitness regimes with the cocktails that would reward them in the evening, after some more creativity of some sort. None of them would come out of this without their cupboards sorted, their house spring cleaned, a new language attempted . . . It was exhausting just listening to it.

There was a breathless energy and speed to all this, a shrillness of enthusiasm, like a bunch of teenage girls getting ready for an outing, convincing each other how much fun they were having. Only, of course, there would not be an outing for quite some time. And they were all over retirement age.

Actually it was difficult to know what age anybody was at the moment. Her book group friends seemed to reside in some adolescent mania, she herself was all of a sudden but persistently identified as elderly, but at the same time being treated like an unreasonable adolescent by her son.

At some stage, she mused, perhaps you had to take on a more parental function with your elderly parents. She had needed to do that for her own mother. Thinking about it now, she might well have been patronising at times, even though her frustration had certainly been rooted in trying to keep her mother safe. One day she could be on the receiving end of this, but surely it would be a gradual process. Or so she had assumed.

Now it seemed to have materialised suddenly. One minute her son had hardly seemed capable of keeping her in mind as another adult with needs and feelings, allowing him to stay in a semi-adolescent country of switching Mum on and off in a perfectly affectionate, but nevertheless completely self-centred way. The next minute he had moved into a position where he showed concern for her welfare, but in a manner that had a caring bossiness and a distinctively patronising tone. Was this the shape of things to come when being vulnerable and elderly robbed you of the option of telling your children to mind their own business?

It was confusing to say the least, this sudden move into a different age category which changed how she saw herself and clearly how her children saw her. In the meantime her book group friends were still dancing on the Titanic, outdoing each other in their positive attitude. There were more WhatsApp messages, but she decided not to open them. She knew what they would say. Loss, what loss? Vulnerabilty? Whose vulnerability? Feeling fear or sadness somehow seemed to have become a failure of character, an indication of low moral immunity. No help when trying to take on board what it might mean to be vulnerable.

In the background on the radio there was a discussion about the latest government briefing, politicians following "the science", the language of shielding, protecting the vulnerable. An angry young man started arguing that the baby boomer generation had not just damaged the planet, benefitted from house price rises, leaving the younger generation with few chances and an enormous task to clear up this mess, but now the entire economy was in free fall as result of the lockdown measures designed to protect that generation.

There was so much anger between the generations and all the shielding and protection of the old people had a dimension to it that did not feel entirely benign. There were scores to be settled here, between her and her son, as there had been between herself and her mother. The tables get turned, the boot is on the other foot now, what went round comes round? Care? Power? Love? These three remain . . . which one was it to be?

She picked up her phone, ignored the WhatsApp book group, and started to write a friendly message to her son, appreciating his concern. Then she looked for the number of her hairdresser.

The Right To Silence
By Angela Rozwadowski

A man glances in my direction, just for a second. Had he held his gaze a little longer, would he have recognised me? Maybe. My hair is shorter now though, bobbed. I'm heavier too. But do my eyes give me away?

A car toots its horn, making me jump. My heart pounds, my hands sweat, my eyes shift from side to side.

An old truck with a rattling exhaust passes, spewing out diesel fumes. They catch the back of my throat and I muffle a cough, keeping my head down. I step backwards and bump into a boy engrossed in his phone. He mutters an apology. He doesn't look up.

I breathe a sigh of relief as I see the familiar yellow car in the slow-moving traffic. Nicky pulls up and I jump into the passenger seat, moving her bag to the floor.

"Morning, Lucy!" Nicky is always cheerful. Full of hope and optimism – characteristics necessary to inspire and cajole ex-cons who invariably see their future down a long, dark tunnel.

I catch a whiff of pine from the wooden balls hanging from her rearview mirror and I think of Tom kicking the leaves in the forest, and then tripping up on a prominent root. I wrap my arms around him. I can taste his salty tears and smell the peanut butter he had for breakfast that morning. I let the image linger for a while.

Nicky's bangles jangle as she changes gear. Like bunches of keys. My heart quickens again. I take a deep breath, close my eyes and slowly exhale.

I notice a pile of sweet wrappers in the pocket of the door. I'm comforted she has a weakness, succumbs to temptation, indulges in the not-so-healthy. I am reassured she is human. But most of all I am glad that the smiling, non-judgemental woman sitting next to me was happy to take me on.

So many wanted to throw away the key after my conviction – reform an unthinkable option for taking a life. I knew that exercising my right to silence could imply guilt.

Nicky indicates left then turns into the car park of Pete's Garden Centre. I completed a horticultural degree in prison and am looking forward to my first day of paid work. Pete had taken on ex-cons before, but Nicky must introduce me and remind us both of the rules. The adjustment will take a while, she says again, as we step out of the car. I will find it strange not asking to use the toilet, wander freely or approach others without threat or confrontation. Nicky smiles, a comforting smile.

We walk up to a wooden hut, the closed door bearing a faded sign *Office*. I peer through the window. Pete isn't here. We wander round the plants and shrubs. The roses, past their best, still exhibit their brightly-coloured heads above glossy green leaves. The scent of the lavender and the large heads of the hydrangea trigger a flutter of excitement in my stomach. I have been counting the years for this moment. And here I am.

A man steps out from behind a row of bamboo. Our eyes meet. I notice his weathered skin, bushy brown hair and steel grey eyes. I hadn't heard his footsteps. Had he been watching me? I feel my heart falter before it resumes its frantic rhythm again.

Nicky breaks the ice. "There you are, Pete."

Pete steps forward holding out his hand. "Pleased to meet you, Lucy." A scowl suggests otherwise. His frown deepens. He nods his head, then tilts it from one side to the other. His visual appraisal of me is so blatant, I want to turn round and run home, back to the safety and security of my bedsit.

After the run-down of rules, Nicky leaves. Pete doesn't move. I can hear his breathing, a subtle wheeze breaking the silence. I fiddle with my hair, put my hands in my pockets, take them out again and look anywhere but his eyes.

"Right, then," he says eventually, with a swing in his voice. "Let's get you to work. Follow me."

I walk behind him. Shuffling along the path, his heavy boots leave a trail of footprints in the gravel. He stops abruptly and hands me a box, saying, "Collect the seeds from the perennials." He gestures around us then leaves, his footsteps retreating like the postman on a frosty morning. I get to work.

I think of that day. I remember it like it was yesterday. The ashen face, the stillness of her body, the emptiness in her eyes. The pillow on her face. Emily was just three weeks old. Tom was watching television, staring at his favourite cartoon characters. There must have been the familiar singing, but I couldn't hear it.

At lunchtime I sit in the corner of the staff room, keeping my eyes to the floor. I speak only when I am spoken to. In prison, I was no contest to the heavy antagonists daring me to make eye contact in the wrong way. It will take time to learn to interpret body language and facial expressions again.

A boy sits opposite me. Too young to recognise me. Sixteen? The same age as Tom is now and I wonder what he is doing. Having his lunch too, perhaps. Does he think of me? I hope he will agree to meet up one day. I have no doubt I would recognise him if I saw him again. His hair might be darker, he will have lost his baby teeth, but smiles never change. I imagine him to be tall, like his dad. He had my eyes, long lashes. And a small scar on his cheek where he fell on the pavement.

The boy stands up and brushes the crumbs from his jumper. He catches my eye and his lips attempt a smile. I nod my head. I imagine he is Tom. I want to rush forward and wrap my arms around him, ruffle his hair and feel the softness of his skin. I want to say I am sorry, but the price of my lie is worth the freedom for my son. I have no regrets.

A Letter
By Ann Means

A large brown envelope, postmarked Dresden. How many years since he'd heard anything from over there? Here he was at the opposite end of the world with the sounds of the bush all around, the sharp scents of dust and eucalyptus, the dappled shade of the afternoon sun. How many years?

It was unusual for him to sit down at this time of day, with the chooks to feed, veggies to water, wood to chop for the cooler nights coming. But this. It took the strength from his legs, for a while.

Inside the brown envelope, another. And a piece of paper too, with a note scrawled in English. They presumably thought after all these years he would have forgotten the language he spoke as a child. 'I hope this finds you. Greetings from your Cousin Gottfried.' No return address.

Cousin Gottfried? No memories of cousins in Dresden. Memories of cousins in the West, yes, of course. Memories of pinchings and kickings, of being reminded over and over again that he was lucky to be taken in, that he should be grateful for scraps and shelter. Memories of scrubbing the workshop floor with cold water and raw red hands, memories of hauling in coal, of thin blankets and thinner food. Memories he thought had gone for good, years ago when he left.

But it was the writing on the envelope, propped up against the teapot, that got to him. You don't see envelopes like that now. Small, cheap paper, barely sealed with browned scotch tape where the gum hadn't stuck. They used to make the gum from boiled animal skins, didn't they? Wasn't that why it had that peculiar acrid smell? The paper was probably whitish once, now it was yellowy-grey.

But . . . that writing. Clear, elegant capitals. And just two words, *Johannes Schneider*. The same words, the same writing. Those words that had been printed on a large piece of paper and pinned to his coat. His father had taken him to the Hauptbahnhof, pointed out the train and reminded him, reminded him again and again, what he had to say if he was questioned.

"I am Johannes Schneider. I have to return to my family in Hannover. This is the address. No, I have no relatives in the German Democratic Republic. I hurt my head and I was in the hospital. My parents have gone home already to work. I want to go home, to Hannover."

Of course he was questioned. A 10-year-old boy, bundled up in winter coat and knitted scarf, short trousers, long grey socks, scuffed black plastic shoes, with a handwritten label on his coat and a small brown cardboard case. In it a shirt, underwear, two more pairs of socks, carefully darned. A small piece of soap and a faded wash cloth. And a greasy paper package with two dry rolls and a precious piece of salami. Nothing else.

The guards didn't know what to do with him. The fat one, who looked like he was calculating the amount of paperwork if they took the boy off the train, eventually said, "Okay, just let him go. Let him go, his family will be waiting."

And now, this letter. Nothing for years. Nothing during all the time when every minute was miserable, every minute with those people who didn't want him. Nothing in the post, no letters smuggled out by others who made that perilous journey from East to West. No phone calls, no messages. Nothing before the day he left for the New World when he was 18. Nothing afterwards. Until now.

A letter from his mother.

What did she have to say to him? What could she have

to say to him, now? Was she still alive? How old would she be? But, this letter was old. It was not from now, it was from then.

Memories came to him. Tall, thin, hair swept up and pinned untidily, bony hand impatiently tugging at a sleeve, crisp clear way of talking, no nonsense. Scrupulous about school work, bedtime, washing face and hands. Children should be seen and not heard. Mama and Papa have important work to do. Those people who visit, they are Mama and Papa's work colleagues. If anyone asks you, you must say you have not seen anyone. Now eat everything on the plate. Go to your room.

What could she say to him now? As he was leaving, she had said he must behave well, he must obey Aunt and Uncle, he must study hard. It was Papa who tried to explain that this was necessary, that it might be hard but it was for the cause, that sometimes Mamas and Papas and children had to endure some hardships. But the cause was good, and in the end it would be alright.

He mustn't say any more and he must never ever tell anyone, here or there, about what Mama and Papa were doing. Not anyone. They were teachers, that was what they did. Nothing else. Their colleagues came to visit to talk about work. That's all. It was Papa who took him to the train, who squeezed his hand so hard it hurt, who sniffed and had watery eyes. "Auf Wiedersehen,

Hansi. Leb wohl." Live well.

And as the screech of the mynahs brought him back to the present, he thought, *Yes, I did live well. I do live well. Here in Australia there was work, a family. And now this place I built by myself, for myself. In the ever-changing never-changing Tasmanian bush. Twice a week on the motorbike up to town to read the papers, meet a friend or two, to pick up the post.*

Today there was a letter. The letter. Johannes Schneider, Hansi, Hans, picked up the envelope. And without opening it, without looking at it again, threw it on the fire.

The Last Meal
By Sheila Gove

"So, son, what would you like for your dinner tonight?" Marshal Tomkins asked, leaning against the bars of my cell.

With nothing to do but think, I'd lately given the matter a whole lot of thought.

"A big juicy steak," I said. "With all the trimmings."

Not that I had any idea what the trimmings were. Hell, I'd never even once had a steak before.

"Apple pie and cream. And an ice-cold beer."

I ain't never had beer before neither. I have drunk whiskey though, forced down my throat for a laugh by the bastard I was meant to call Pa.

"Fair enough. And son, d'you want the priest to sit with you tonight?"

"Hell, no!" I didn't have no time for religion since I went to the priest of our local church for help. "It's God's will," he'd said. He did nothing for Ma and me, being like everyone else and not wanting to interfere between a woman and her husband.

And in the end, Ma had done nothing for *me*. She hadn't stood by me. Hadn't visited me since the trial.

I'd never known my real Pa. He lit out for places unknown before I was born. Maybe that was why Ma didn't much like me, blaming me for ruining her life. See, her God-fearing family threw her out once they knew she was carrying a kid.

She'd moved away, ending up in a dusty town in Kansas where she called herself Mrs Johnson and said she was a widow – Mr Johnson having gone to California and been slain by a band of Sioux on the way. If people didn't believe her they didn't say nothing. Frontier folk don't ask about anyone's past.

Was Johnson my real Pa's name? Maybe she just used it cos it sounded okay.

For 14 years it had been just Ma and me. She took in washing and soon as I was old enough, I did odd jobs. A fair few folk were willing to employ me, skinny and small though I always was. Probably they didn't feel the need to pay me a fair price for my work.

We lived hand to mouth so we sure couldn't afford steak and apple pie. Some nights we could hardly afford biscuits and beans.

I guess I felt okay about things, not knowing

anything different, until Hell turned up in the shape of Bill Winslow.

Ma allowed herself to be charmed by him. I could understand why. He was good-looking with his dark brown hair, moustache and blue eyes. Tall and broad with it. And he had a way with him. Until he didn't.

I could never understand what he saw in her. He could've had his pick of women all younger and prettier than her and with more money too. But within weeks of them meeting they were standing up before the priest and saying their marriage vows.

What he saw in me was a punchbag. From the moment he laid his eyes on me he had no time for me – nor me him, come to that. It weren't long before he was using his fists and his feet and belt to wallop me.

Most Saturday nights he'd go drinking and come home stinking of bad whiskey and cigarette smoke. That was when he took his rages out on Ma as well.

Usually it started over his dinner. It was too hot or too cold. Burnt. Raw. It didn't matter none that the fault was his because he'd gotten home late. Nothing was ever his fault. It was mine for being a bastard or Ma's for being a stupid bitch or common whore.

One time he threw a plate of stew on the kitchen floor and made me lick it up. Ma stood by wringing her hands, waiting for him to give her another black eye or cracked rib.

I guess his temper would've ended up with one of us dead at his hands and him here instead of me if things had gone on that way.

But soon after my sixteenth birthday I walked into town and there in Mr Dempsey's store window was a Colt six-shooter. My heart thumped to see it. As the saying goes, 'God made all men, Samuel Colt made all men equal'. With that gun I'd be equal to Winslow even though I was so much smaller than him. But don't go thinking I got me that gun and shot him dead. Of course I didn't. I could never have afforded it with what I earned.

Did give me an idea though.

I had a knife, a piece of wood was easy to come by and I could whittle. I whittled away until I had a stick as long and sharp and pointed as a stick could be.

A few weeks later, the bastard came home loaded for bear. He'd lost at poker. Stupid sonofabitch never was no good at cards and had to cheat to win. This time he'd been seen palming two aces – him not being much good at cheating either. So he lost all his money and they'd tossed him out of the saloon onto his sorry ass, everyone laughing at him.

As soon as Ma placed his dinner on the table he started yelling. Words I don't wanna repeat. He picked up the plate and threw it and the beans at her. She cried and begged like she always did, for all the good it did her, and cowered in the corner. She cried harder when he began to take off his belt.

"Leave her be!" I shouted.

The bastard turned round and looked at me and laughed to see me standing there, waving that sharp stick in front of me.

"What you going to do with that, boy?" he sneered. "You ain't got the guts."

He could see my hand was shaking bad.

"You'll get yours after I've dealt with your useless Ma."

He turned back to Ma and swung the belt, bringing the buckle down hard on her arm. She was screaming in pain and I leapt on his back and stuck that stick as hard as I could into his goddamn neck.

"You, you!" he was roaring with pain and fury.

He shook me off and I backed away terrified. Shit! I hadn't killed him. How could he not be dead? He'd kill me instead, then Ma too probably, with the temper he was in. With one hand he grabbed my jacket and with the other he pulled out the stick.

There was a puzzled, furious look on his face when he hit the floor, covered with all his own redness. He drummed his heels a couple of times, didn't move again.

"Ma," I said. "Come on." I'd hoped she would run away with me. We could go to Arizona and start up in the cattle busines or maybe strike silver in Colorado. I could see now that was even more of an impossible dream than it had ever been.

She just screamed. "What have you done?" Then, "Bill! My Bill!" She threw herself down beside the bastard, cradling his lifeless body, weeping over the man who'd misused the both of us. God, but it was hard to see: Ma preferred the man who knocked her about to me, her only son, who'd done for him.

I took off. But I'd gotten no more than 20 miles when the posse led by Marshal Tomkins caught up. Brought me back to stand trial for the unlawful killing of my stepfather.

I could've been granted some sort of clemency. Even though, when the judge asked me if I regretted what I'd done, I said no. Even though no one spoke up for me, not the priest and not one none of the neighbours who knew the truth.

Then Ma got up in the witness box and said what a wonderful husband Bill Winslow had been and how I'd murdered him because I was a wicked, sinful boy jealous of their happiness.

That settled my hash.

Guilty. Hanged by the neck until dead.

I wonder whether Ma, or our priest, will be there to see me walk to the gallows. And find I don't much care either way.

So later this evening Marshal Tomkins brought me that big juicy steak with fried tomatoes and potatoes and something he called squash. Did it smell good. And the beer was frothing over the top of the glass.

"You know, son," he said with a sigh. "Sometimes this here job don't seem up to much. I'm real sorry about this. I wish it could be otherwise." He shook his head. "Ain't fair. Kid like you."

"It's alright," I said. "I don't mind."

I could tell he didn't believe me. But it's true.

Finale
By Steve Ward

Applause fades to a murmur as the curtain drops behind him. *Finis.* Grotesque shadows of ring boys are thrown against the canvas wall separating him from ring side. Safe in the sanctuary of his make-up tent he is relieved of the noise and the smell. That mawkish mixture of popcorn, candy floss, and the acrid pungency of animals that seems to have permeated his skin over the years; the smell *del circo.*

He crosses to the simple wooden chair and flops onto it. He is drained, spent, empty. Years of endless slapstick and prat-falls are beginning to take their toll. His feet throb. With the effort of age he loosens the laces of his over-sized shoes, before kicking them off and wriggling his toes in relief. He studies them as they lie there forlorn on the damp grass, absurd symbols of his life's art.

The band strikes up as the chattering audience begins

to depart; twinkle-eyed children clutching a parent in one hand and a candy floss in the other, their heads full of wondrous sights and sounds. He half listens for a moment.

Striking a match, he lights the wax-encrusted candle stub and looks into the mirror propped up on the table. *So tired.* In the guttering light the face before him grimaces and the red hair stands up on end; the hair that has sent so many children into shrieks of delight. Slowly he pulls it from his head and drops it into its small suitcase. It lies there like some abandoned exotic creature waiting to be fed. He looks at it for a moment, prods it with his toe as if expecting it to move, and then runs his hands over his head and stares back into the mirror.

His make-up seems even more garish set against the short, silver-grey hair. Would children still love him if he appeared like this, or would they be scared? Would they even recognise him? He pulls the red nose from his face, leaving an incongruous flesh-coloured blob surrounded by a patchwork of white make-up, exaggerated eyes and mouth.

No, he thinks, it's definitely the hair that makes him who he is. The children love it when his hair stands on end, seemingly of its own accord. Even the adults laugh – sometimes. Why? Do they see something of themselves in him? Do they feel his embarrassment, his fear? Do they know? Or do they see simply a man in a silly wig?

He sighs, it's getting late. It's simple really – without his hair he is nothing, just another clown to them. He bridles. No, not a clown – he is an Auguste! *So tired.* From a jar on the table he scoops a handful of cream and begins to lather his face. The image in the mirror becomes distorted, colours begin to smear together. He traces patterns with his fingers and with each pass of the hand a new face appears, mocking him in his search for his true self. He pauses and studies the mirror hard. He is in there somewhere.

He begins to wipe the make-up from his face. First one eye, then the other. He looks into the mirror again, and as he does so a child's face emerges before him. He blinks. It is still there. A small chubby-faced boy with unruly hair and round National Health glasses. The boy grins at him. Is this his inner child? A distant memory sparks somewhere in his brain. How old would he have been then? Four? Five?

He closes his eyes and is transported back to a birthday treat to the circus, sitting between his mother and his grandmother. Ring side seats in a vast tented cathedral. His senses are overwhelmed; the lights and colour; the sound of brassy music, the smell of sawdust and damp grass. A magical world unfolds before him; anthracite-shiny nodding-plumed horses, soaring super-humans, yellow-fanged nightmare beasts – and the clown.

The clown, alone in the centre of the ring, master of that hallowed space, who looks directly at him as his hair rises magically on either side of his head. Copper red hair. He feels himself being plucked from his seat and carried to the centre of the ring. Was he terrified, excited? He can't remember.

The clown marks a cross in the sawdust and gestures. The boy stands on it. No words are needed, he seems to know exactly what is required of him. The clown gestures again and the audience applauds. He stares out at the crowd, vague darkened shapes beyond a veil of bright lights. He knows that all eyes are looking at him. A cap is fitted to his head and he smells the stale popcorn sweetness of the clown as he bends over him. He breathes it in, intoxicating, exciting.

The clown produces a cup and saucer from deep within the folds of his jacket and places them on the flat pad of the cap and signs for him to be absolutely still. He feels the clown magic a tea-spoon from behind his ear. He dare not look round, even though the audience laughs and applauds. They are laughing at him, applauding him. He is the centre of their attention, there in the ring. He is a performer. The clown bends down and places the tea-spoon on the toe of his enormous shoe and with one deft movement flicks it into the air. It spins and glints in the light before falling into the tea-cup with a tinkle.

The crowd roars its approval and the boy grins widely, eyes sparkling. Another tea-spoon appears, and then another, from all parts of his body. With each spoon the applause and laughter grows, and as each is successfully tossed into the tea-cup he feels himself growing in stature. With an expansive gesture the clown makes a bow and signals the boy to do the same. He does, and the spoons cascade out of the tea-cup onto the soft sawdust beneath his feet.

The audience laughs as the boy continues to bow, turning left and then right to acknowledge them all. He is playing to the crowd. He has sawdust in his shoes. The clown applauds him, this podgy, short baggy-trousered child, and points him to his seat but still he bows, revelling in the moment. In feigned consternation the clown sinks to his knees.

His hair rises and he clasps his hands together in supplication before the boy, as he gestures again to his seat in the crowd. The boy stands firm and throws his arms wide, as if to embrace the laughter. He feels himself being picked up as the clown scoops him up under one arm and carries him back to his seat. The clown walks back to the centre of the ring and turns to look at him. His hair rises again as a final salute.

He opens his eyes and looks again into the mirror.

He is suddenly aware that he is crying. *So tired.* The distant clown raises one hand and waves, and he waves back as the figure slowly dims and fades to blackness.

. . .

Finale for Veste

It is with great sadness that we report the death of the renowned veteran clown Veste. Veste, who had brought laughter to generations of circus audiences, was discovered in his make-up tent after the final show of the season of Circus Pellagrini. He died peacefully doing the work he had always loved.

A Winter's Tale
By Ellen Evers

It was the unexpectedness that did for me. Who'd think you would hear a Christmas song in September? It was in that charity shop just down from Piccadilly, you know the one we always popped into on our way to the station. You indulged me, Harvey Nicks was more your scene, but it was fun wasn't it, rooting round for trash or treasure? I was in there for old times' sake and hearing that was like a punch in the stomach.

When I returned from my sentimental journey, the first thing I did was play that track, over and over. The song that had become ours. Pathetic, I know. When I'd sickened myself of David's plaintive notes, I wallowed again by looking at your picture.

I'm not sure exactly when we both discovered a mutual love of David Essex; it must have come up in conversation I suppose. You showed me that photo taken so long ago with the young, dark and gorgeous David and I was frankly very jealous indeed. Living on the Isle of Wight while they filmed *That'll be the Day* and being one of the extras was your claim to fame. You were wearing hot pants showing off your long legs with fabulous high wedges; your hair glossy black, your mouth a pout. No wonder he wanted to drape his famous arms around you. You laughed and made some wry comment on how the years had taken their toll on all of us.

Years pass, don't they? But, although you would never agree, I think you are as beautiful now as you were all those years ago. I can see you shaking your head. We agree to differ on that. But you let me keep the picture.

Do you remember what we talked about that first time at the gym? I must admit I don't, but before we knew it, we were meeting up for coffee and then running on a regular basis. That's when we found we loved the cold; that morning when the rest of the runners took one look at the weather and headed back indoors for hot chocolate, we couldn't wait to get out there.

I always felt that I'd been the only person looking forward to darker nights, colder weather and all the stuff that comes with winter – until I met you. I don't include Christmas in that of course; we were united in our overwhelming dislike of the season. 'Always winter and never Christmas.' That Narnia quotation appealed to us as something to be embraced, not feared. It was another bond that defined us. That was when I knew I was falling in love with you.

I soon guessed that you were well off. Not that you made a big deal of it. Thank you for that. I do have my pride as you know. That first skiing trip was wonderful and I will never forget it although it was a miracle we survived with no broken bones. You surprised me when you said you'd never been skiing before, it seemed so your sort of thing. When you told me your late husband didn't want to go I didn't understand why that meant you couldn't do it. But hey, I've never been married so what would I know?

That winter everyone complained about the snow that came in November and stayed through December but we loved every bit of it especially as your family were all snow bound in Scotland and couldn't come to see you for weeks. I know it sounds selfish but that suited me, and I could have you all to myself. I think you knew what their reaction to us would be even then, but we didn't talk about it.

Instead, we walked with poles and heavy boots through the silent snow – talking of everything and nothing. It didn't matter. Then back to my tiny terraced house where we'd shower and sit curled up in front of a real log fire, having a real girly night in.

We went to your place sometimes, I know, but we

both felt my discomfort despite the perfect luxury of the house. I felt the family presence although you laughed at me for being so fanciful. "What they don't know won't hurt them," you said and of course you were right.

We watched every film David ever made and cried every time he died in *Silver Dream Racer*. You told stories of making *your film*, as we dubbed it, what fun that was and how you admired David. You even met him again years later after one of his shows and you said he pretended to remember you. Pretended? I don't think so. You admitted though to being depressed at greeting an old man when all your memories were of youth.

Thank God the drifts were up to the top of hedges in Scotland and you told those daughters who lived in the Highlands that you were fine and spending Christmas with an old friend. We giggled at the word *old*; we felt like kids. Why didn't you admit to them that you'd always hated Christmas?

We had an alternative Christmas and it was magical; well at first, and it was ours. The much-promised white Christmas brought the usual traffic chaos but it didn't bother us. We bought in all our favourite food with champagne and Australian merlot, banked up the fire and put on David's hits. I thought it was perfect until you started to cry at the end of *A Winter's Tale* and despite hugs and shushing I just couldn't make you stop; you were breaking your heart and I didn't know why.

"It's the words, they're so sad. They could be written for us."

I knew the lyrics. I didn't know you felt like this but you pulled yourself together, laughed and said something about too much red wine making you maudlin. I went along with it but I could feel the change.

Too soon the thaw came with floods and milder weather. Your family planned a trip down south to spend New Year with you. They were insistent, you couldn't put them off you said and I believed you. I was to be introduced as a special friend. What you had not told me was that you had written to prepare them for your news; to tell them that you wanted us to move in together, as a couple. Not surprisingly they were down here like a shot. Liberal-minded they were until their mother was involved. You knew what their reaction was at Christmas didn't you? No wonder David made you cry.

I can't even think about that evening and how I felt – an intruder, interloper. You changed too; your daughters ganged up on you and you lost your nerve. I couldn't wait to get out. You see, I've nothing to lose – no family – nobody to judge me.

But you couldn't do it, could you? They implied I was only after your money and your house. They were very persuasive and made you cry and cry again. And I was too stubborn to fight them. They made you feel ashamed.

And so, you are living in Scotland, the land of winter snows which you will love. You can even go skiing as long as the family approve. Sorry, you don't deserve that. Or maybe you do.

I didn't reply to your emails. What could I say? You had made up your mind and I wasn't going to beg. But I just wanted to tell you that that winter was the happiest time of my life. I'm okay so don't worry about me. The CDs and DVDs have got to go, though. I'm taking them to the charity shop near Piccadilly which seems the right place.

I can't listen to David anymore.

Marty
By Andy Stewart

I've known Marty most of my life. From early childhood we've been bosom buddies. We used to play for hours losing all track of time, building rickety dens in the bottom of the garden out of bits of sacking, old boards and plastic sheets. We hid in those shelters from the space monsters, pirates and dinosaurs – and my mum. We'd ward off all invaders using dustbin lids as shields and brooms as swords.

We climbed trees, falling out of many of them. Our knees became scarred as the result of our adventures. We went scrumping in the the neighbour's garden. Poor Mr Kessel with his thick-lensed glasses and white stick, I doubt if he noticed whether there was fruit on the trees or not. I felt a bit guilty about taking advantage of the old bugger, but Marty said he expected Mr Kessel did exactly the same thing when he was our age. And in the evenings we went out into the street next to ours, pressing the doorbells and running away on our stick-like legs, screeching with peals of good-to-be-alive laughter as howls of annoyance rang in our ears.

The highlight of our year was bonfire night, November 5. It was a wonderful community knees-up on the playing fields, with an overdose of sparks, bangs and explosions. We'd chuck potatoes wrapped in foil into the smouldering base of the bonfire and retrieve them after half an hour with the aid of a long stick. Opening up the foil with our gloved hands, we'd split the sizzling spuds into halves, chuck liberal knobs of Anchor on top and enjoy the butter dripping down our chins. I have never tasted anything quite so wonderful. I'll gloss over the time Maudie Frantom's pet tortoise got accidentally barbequed, as Marty insensitively observed to the sobbing Maudie, it was a daft place to choose to hibernate. On the way home Marty would always lob a few jumping jacks through random letterboxes.

They do say that opposites attract. In many ways Marty and I are the same, in others we're like chalk and cheese. For a start, he is always cheerful with a ready grin. Me, I'm more of a serious person, prone to feeling low and riddled with self-doubt. I guess he takes me out of myself. But two things we definitely have in common. We're both only children and each of us has an absentee father. We have agreed not to use the Dad word in our heart-to-hearts. Oh, and we both support Chelsea. "Come on you Blues," we chant as one.

I was always shy. Blushing for England. I wouldn't have said boo to the most timid goose. Marty was the one who went into the newsagent to buy the dodgy top-shelf magazines that we used to take onto the wasteland behind the brewery.

It was Marty who took me into the lounge bar of the George and Dragon to have my first pint of brown ale. I was sick afterwards. My mother thought I had a stomach bug and I got the next day off school.

And when we became teenagers it was Marty who asked the girls to dance, me who wanted to shuffle self-consciously in the shadows. Inevitably it was he who crossed the threshold of our local pharmacy to purchase the inaugural packet of condoms. Left to me they would have stayed in my wallet until well past their use-by-date along with the crumpled five-pound notes and my provisional driving licence.

Marty was a showman. The trick he performed with the condom never failed to delight and fascinate his appreciative audience in the George and Dragon. I know for a fact he rehearsed it for hours until it was perfect.

He would stretch the rubber until it could go over the top of his Brylcreemed hair and his forehead. Once it was covering his ears and his nose, Marty inhaled deeply through his mouth and forced the air out through his nostrils. He inflated it like a balloon until it bulged above his forehead in a latex dome. The climax, to wild applause, had it bursting with a loud bang that sounded like a car backfiring. Marty would remove the broken fragments from his head, milking the laughter before taking a theatrical bow.

There was a darker side to Marty. When the red mist descended. He could get aggressive and inappropriate, paws all over other blokes' girlfriends, and the racist stuff that came out of his mouth made me shudder.

. . .

I had been so proud of my little car. It was an ancient Mini. Chelsea blue with white stuck-on racing stripes. I bought it with money I managed to put aside from my wages at the brewery. I washed and polished it every Sunday morning until it gleamed with a showroom shine. It was always me who drove, I was the one with the licence. Passed my test first time. In truth, I was relieved there was something I could do better than Marty. Even if it was the only thing. And he was more than happy to use me as his bloody chauffeur.

We were coming out of the pub one Saturday lunchtime. As we approached the Mini, we saw a traffic warden sticking a ticket on the windscreen. He wasn't much older than us. A pleasant-looking black guy. He spoke with a soft Brummie accent.

"Sorry, mate. Your meter ran out an hour ago. I've passed by twice, but my supervisor is on the prowl so I had to issue a ticket."

"Why don't you sod off back to where you came from?"

I winced at the vicious vocabulary. I'm a live-and-let-live sort of person. If I had a motto it would be, 'Keep a low profile and stay out of trouble'.

I knew what was coming next. But I couldn't stop him. When Marty was like this, he scared me.

He moved towards the retreating warden, hitting him full force with his right fist on the point of his jaw. There was a loud crack and the man's neck moved like a pile of dislodged plates. He staggered backwards and hit his head on the meter. He fell to the pavement, his eyes glazed over, blood oozing down his face. Then he started convulsing, like he was doing a horizontal break dance. I stood stock still, couldn't move, as if someone had pressed the pause button.

It was busy that Saturday. A patrol car was stuck in a traffic jam just yards away from us. Within seconds two uniformed police officers were beside the felled traffic warden. A crowd had gathered. One man pointed a finger at me.

"It was him. I saw him land the punch."

I started to protest my innocence. I looked around in panic. There was no sign of Marty. He had vanished.

The traffic warden never regained consciousness. The hospital turned off the life-support machine two weeks later. So here I am, serving a murder sentence for a crime I didn't commit.

Every visiting day I keep hoping Marty will turn up to see me. You stick by your pals, don't you? Especially a soul mate. But he never comes. I'm sure he wants to. My Dad disowned me long ago, so he won't bother. In any case, we were never close, even when I was a toddler.

And Mum took an overdose, so I can't see her until she's feeling stronger. Nobody from the pub or the brewery visits. It was Marty they liked.

The psychiatrist says Marty doesn't exist. That I have Dissociative Identity Disorder. A split personality. That's why I'm serving my time in Broadmoor with no release date.

I'm aware someone has entered my cell.

"That bloody bitch of a psychiatrist. This is all her fault. You leave her to me . . . "

The Phone Call
By Peter Johnstone

"Hello."

"Hello, is that . . . Paul?"

"Yes, it's me. Hello, Joan. This is a surprise! How are you?"

"Why aren't you here?"

"Sorry?"

"Why aren't you here? You said you'd be here today."

"Erm, because it's Saturday and I don't arrive until Tuesday."

"What day is it today?"

"It's Saturday . . ."

"And when do you arrive?"

"On Tuesday."

"Let me look at my calendar. What day is it today?"

"It's Saturday."

"The twelfth?"

"No, it's the fifth."

"The fifth?"

"Yes, Saturday, the fifth."

"And, you arrive . . . on Tuesday."

"Yup, that's it."

"The eighth?"

"That's right."

"I've got it written down here, *Paul arriving on Tuesday.*"

"Good."

"And you leave on Saturday, the twelfth."

"That's it"

"And you're coming here on Friday."

"Right."

"Oh dear, I'm so sorry. I'm really sorry"

"Why's that?"

"I get muddled up. I'm so sorry. What must you think of me?"

"It's OK. We all mix up dates."

"But I'm so embarrassed."

"There's no need to be. It's fine. Everybody mixes up dates once in a while."

"Can we go through it again?"

"Of course."

"You arrive on . . ."

"Tuesday."

"On Tuesday. At what time?"

"About nine."

"In the evening?"

"Yes, in the evening."

"That's right. I've got it written down here on my calendar, *Paul arrives, evening.*"

"That's it."

"And you`re staying with Mike."

"You've got it."

"And . . .you're leaving on Saturday."

"That's it, and I'll have lunch with you on Friday."

"Let me write that down. *Lunch with Paul.* . . Oh, I already have. It's written down here."

"Good, you usually write everything down."

"I'm sorry. Can we go through this just one more time?"

"All right."

"You arrive on . . .which day do you arrive on?"

"Tuesday."

"Tuesday the . . ."

"Eighth."

"Do you have any idea when you'll arrive?"

"In the evening, about half past eight or nine, depending on the train connections."

"And then you're . . ."

"Staying with Mike."

"And I'll see you on . . ."

"Friday."

"Any idea what time?"

"Lunch time. I'll bring something light to eat."

"And you leave on . . ."

"Saturday."

"Saturday. That's right, I've got it on my calendar."

"Good. I'm pleased it's all straight."

"Paul?"

"Yes?"

"I want to ask you something."

"Okay. What do you want to ask?"

"Well, er . . . Are you sure you want to come?"

"Of course, I do. It's your eighty-fourth birthday. I wouldn't miss it for the world."

"I get so confused."

"It's okay. It's only sometimes, and we've known each other a long time."

"Over 30 years."

"It's nearly 40 years since we were teaching together."

"Is it that long? Where has the time gone?"

"Do you remember the Old Time Music Hall?"

"How could I forget? Now what did I sing?"

Paul breaks into song, *Let the great big world . . .*

Joan takes over, *Keep turning. Never mind if I've got you . . .*

They sing together. Paul, who does not remember the words, fills in with "La, la, la," while Joan continues,

For I only know, That I want you so.

She tremulously sings the last line alone, *And there's no one else will do.*

There's a long pause before Paul breaks the silence, "And Penny and Katie dressed up as showgirls."

"Yes, and that little lad . . ."

". . . who did that Stanley Holloway piece from memory."

"Kevin!"

"That's him! On his 'orse, with his 'awk . . ."

". . . in his 'and."

"Brought the house down."

"It was a wonderful night."

"It was amazing. I'm really looking forward to seeing you again."

"I am too. When are you arriving?"

"I'm arriving in England on Tuesday"

"That's the . . ."

"The eighth."

"Tuesday."

"Yes, Tuesday the eighth."

"That's right. Here it is. *Paul arrives on Tuesday the eighth.*"

"Yup."

"Do you know what time?"

"In the evening around nine."

"You're staying with Mike?"

"That's it."

"You'll be here on Friday. Any idea when?"

"About lunchtime"

"Let me write that down, *A–bout–lunch–time*."

"Good."

"And, you're leaving on Saturday."

"That's it. Look, I'll phone you on Monday to confirm the arrangements."

"But you usually phone on Tuesday."

"I know, but I won't be there, because I'll be travelling."

"Oh, so when are you arriving?"

"On Tuesday, but I'll phone you on Monday so that everything is clear. Sorry, Joan but I've got to go. I've got the shopping to unpack. Best wishes for your birthday. See you soon."

"But what day are you coming?"

"I'm coming on . . . why don't you look at your calendar and tell me what you've written."

"What date is that?"

"The eighth."

"On Tuesday."

"Yes, that's it. Tuesday the eighth."

"Any idea when?"

"What have you written on your calendar?"

"Erm . . . Ah, Tuesday the eighth, *Paul arrives in the*

evening."

"That's right."

"And you're staying with Mike."

"Yes."

"And, I'll see you on . . ."

"What does it say on the calendar?"

"Wait a moment. Here it is. *Lunch with Paul on Friday.*"

"Very good."

"And, you leave on Saturday."

"That's it. You've got it. But I really have to go. Have a lovely birthday party with your family, Joan. See you on Friday. Lots of love. Bye."

. . .

He puts the phone down quickly, reaches into the shopping bags and opens the fridge door to put milk and cheese in. The phone rings. He stares at it and lets it ring three of four times before answering.

"Hi, Joan."

"Hello? Paul?"

"Yes, it's me."

"How did you know it was me?"

"I had a feeling it might be."

"I wanted to ask you about when you're coming."

"Okay, just give me a few moments to pull up a chair and make myself comfortable, then we'll go through it."

Time Pays No Heed
By Barbara Gurney

On my way to the train
There was a man sitting on a bench.
I hurried by.

On my way to the train
There was a man sitting on a bench on a veranda.
I glanced at him.

On my way to the train
There was a man sitting on a bench on a veranda, a dog
at his side.
I nodded.

On my way to the train
There was a man sitting on a bench on a veranda, a dog at
his side, a scarf around his neck.
I smiled.

On my way to the train
There was a man sitting on a bench on a veranda, a dog at his side, a scarf around his neck, a book on his lap.
I waved.

On my way to the train
There was a man sitting on a bench on a veranda, a dog at his side, a scarf around his neck, a book on his lap, a cup of tea in his hand.
I said hello.

On my way to the train
There was a man sitting on a bench on a veranda, a dog at his side, a scarf around his neck, a book on his lap, a cup of tea in his hand, a walking stick leaning against the bench.
I mentioned the weather.

On my way to the train there was a man sitting on a bench on a veranda, a dog at his side, a scarf around his neck, a book on his lap, a cup of tea in his hand, a walking stick leaning against the bench, a rug over his knee.
I stopped.

The dog came down to the picket fence, barking a greeting.

"Hi, puppy," I said, even though the dog had a grey muzzle and walked slowly.

It put two hairy black paws on the horizontal beam.

The doggy grin encouraged me to ruffle its fur and stroke its ears.

"What's the dog's name?"

The man placed his cup on the concrete floor, patted his knee as he called the dog, "Here, boy." He waited for the dog to come to his side. "Buster. And I'm trying to train him not to bark at everyone who goes by."

"Oh, I'm sorry."

"That's okay. You're our regular. It's nice to have regulars, don't you think?"

I laughed. "Like old friends, you mean?"

"Exactly," he replied.

We chatted about the memories created by watching the children on the other side of the road riding their bicycles, presumably going to school. I told him he'd better drink his tea before it got cold. He reminded me I had a train to catch.

On my way to the train there was a man sitting on a bench on a veranda, a dog at his side, a scarf around his neck, a book on his lap, a cup of tea in his hand, a walking stick leaning on the bench, a rug over his knee.

"Nice scarf," I said.

"Knitted by my favourite granddaughter."

"Do you have many grandchildren?"

He chuckled, which ended in a coughing fit. While he recovered, I patted Buster and let him lick my hand.

"Only the one," he said.

"That's cute. I bet I'm your favourite passer-by who catches the train every morning at eight, who wears a ridiculous orange sun-hat, and is always running late because she stops and chats to you."

"Indeed."

"Are they your football team colours?"

They weren't, but we spoke at length about coaches, umpires, pampered players and how neither of us had been to a game.

"I better go. The train won't wait."

"No," he said. "Time pays no heed."

"Only rushes to the end," I said.

"See you tomorrow."

I agreed.

At the corner I turned and waved again.

On my way to the train
There was no man sitting on the bench on the veranda
No dog to be at his side
No book for reading
No tea cup, no walking stick or rug for his knee
Just a lonely bench with a scarf and a lily.
I lingered.
I cried.

The train came anyway.

Biographies

The Other Pianist   **David Allard**

I live in North London and have had a stellar non-career as a dairy herdsman, soldier, gardener, television programme salesman, sales director and financial director (none of these simultaneously). Inspiration comes from small, observed scenes and then imagination takes over – if good fortune is there.

Scarlet Lipstick   **Angela Aries**

After many years of teaching and co-authoring textbooks, Angela is delighted to have more time to devote to fiction. She is particularly interested in writing historical novels, and loves doing the necessary research. She hopes to complete her Roman trilogy shortly. In her spare time she enjoys singing, and gardening.

Vulnerable   **Annette Byford**

Annette grew up in Germany and came to the UK in her late 20s. She is married with two children and two grandchildren. She works as a psychotherapist and is interested in the dynamics of parenting adult children. She has published a book on the family dynamics of weddings.

The Sense of You   **Richard Copestake**
At 12 I wanted to be the next Fleming. Instead at 16
I started an engineering career and travelled the world.
No regrets – all those reports honed structure, research
and narrative skills. Since retiring to Suffolk I've had
success with freelance features. Fiction remains a work
in progress.

Bubbles   **Michael Coutts**
I am married, live in Edinburgh and we have three
daughters. I used to be a scientist working on the
physiology of trees. After retiring in 1995 I had more time
for painting (see michaelcoutts.com) and took a course in
creative writing. I particularly enjoy creating characters
and writing dialogue.

Sophie   **Dorothy Cox**
I have always been an avid reader and have been a letter-
writer for many years. I came late to story writing and
enjoy it far more than I expected. I wish I had started years
ago! I have had some short stories published and have
been successful in several competitions.

Hands   **Michael Dixon**

Now retired, I worked variously as a tax officer, teacher and immigration officer. Originally from South Wales, I taught in Tanzania for two years and spent most of my adult life in England. Married to Jayne, with four children, nine grandchildren and four chihuahuas.

See You at Twilight   **Michael Downes**

I live in Victoria, Australia, though I was born and raised in Ireland. I have been writing for over 40 years. To date, I have written four novels, many novellas, novelettes, and short stories, and collected prizes along the way. My latest novel, *The Portal In The Attic*, was published in 2021.

A Winter's Tale   **Ellen Evers**

I'm a 70-something retired teacher who enjoys writing short stories, non-fiction and occasionally poetry. When I'm not writing I like walking and keeping fit, being with my family and lots of travel. I love history and enjoy being a tour guide which sometimes inspires my writing!

Thursday's Shepherd's Pie   **Mandy Fouracre**

I have scribbled on and off for years as a means of expressing ideas, thoughts and characters that bubble away in my imagination. This is the first time I have entered a writing competition. It was a complete shock (but also encouraging) to learn that my scribblings were read and appreciated.

The Last Meal   **Sheila Gove**

I am retired and live in East Devon. Interested in the American West, I have been published as an author of Black Horse Westerns. I enjoy writing short stories and am trying to write crime fiction. I belong to a writing group.

Time Pays No Heed   **Barbara Gurney**

Barbara lives in Perth, Western Australia. She writes fiction for adults and children and free verse poetry. Barbara enjoys creating memorable characters and exposing life experiences – often of the ordinary person. The unconscious creative voices haven't finished with her yet! Her newest novel, *Doors of Prague*, appeared in 2021. www.barbaragurney.com

Bartlett, the Dog and the Old Sailor   **Ron Hardwick**

Ron is a retired head of procurement who has been writing short fiction for half a century, He has been married for 48 years and has one son and a grandson. He lives in Scotland and his one remaining ambition is to see his accountant-turned-private detective Mr Lemon stories published.

Our Aftermath   **Marion Horton**

I have been writing sporadically for several years, but only recently begun sharing my work. I have discovered writing is an addiction – once you have begun you'll see possibilities in everything. I live in Sussex where my pen twitches in anticipation – what will I see today?

Life in Lines   **Linda Hurdwell**

My previous work involving learning disabilities is often included in my writing. These people are very dear to me and I want to help people understand their dilemmas more. I am a widow with a lovely cocker spaniel and two adult sons. I live in a country village, where my dog and I have lovely walks. Writing helps me survive.

Harry's Chair   **Cathy Ives**
I write, therefore I am – despite being slightly dyslexic. In the past I have written poems, short stories and one-act plays which have been performed. I also currently run a local writing group.

The Phone Call   **Peter Johnstone**
I have dabbled in writing for years. The ambition to write a great novel is now reduced to letters to friends, complaints to tax collectors and rambling essays about my life. At the age of 74, I am delighted to have *The Phone Call* included here. The story is in memory of an ex-colleague.

Amid the Winter Snow   **Donovan Laurie**
A scientist by training, I spent half my working life in the world of education – in schools and colleges. In my 40s, I retrained and became an Anglican vicar. On retirement I joined a U3A writing group and am now rarely seen without a pencil and paper thinking up my next story!

The House in Montmartre   **Peter Lewis**
I'm a retired teacher who loves to write. My other passion
is France and when not there I write stories set in France.
I've also self-published a novel, *A Snowfox in Normandy*.
My story *A Winter's Tale* was included in *WriteTime
ONE* and I'm delighted to have another this time.

Delete   **Laurel Lindström**
Laurel Lindström has had a long and rewarding career as a
technical writer and journalist. Under the name of Laurel
Brunner she specialises in digital prepress, printing and
publishing technologies and her work has been published
all over the world. Laurel is married to Paul and together
they have three grown up children.

The Housesitter   **Angela Lombardo**
Angela is active in her writing community and has
read essays at Live Lit events sponsored by The Irish
American Heritage Center, Chicago. Her story, *Janet
Was the Girl*, was published by Flash Fiction Magazine,
December, 2015. *The Rhinestone Pin* was published by
East On Central Literary Magazine, November, 2018.

A Walk in the Park   **Brian McDonald**

I left school in 1969 with no qualifications to speak of and worked in a chemical factory, as a psychiatric nurse, soap packer and cornflake maker before spending 20 years as a housing officer in North Manchester. Now I write, swim and watch Manchester City. This story is for fearless Dorrie.

The Monkey Puzzle Tree   **Gwenda Major**

I live in the Lake District and was a teacher of deaf children. I have two children and four grandchildren and my interests include genealogy, gardens and graveyards. I have been lucky to have had many short stories published but I'm still dreaming of having one of my novels published.

A Letter   **Ann Means**

Ann now lives in Oxford after 20 years of living and working overseas. She loves travel, reading, walking, conversation, and is learning to sing. And of course she enjoys writing, from limericks and nonsense poems to book reviews and short stories.

The Life of Riley   **Chris Milner**

Chris, from Hexham in Northumberland, has spent a lifetime getting older and now enjoys trying to fit his impressive collection of memories and other stuff into stories. He isn't as fit as once he was, much prefers letters to emails and fears the climate is beyond saving.

Cody's Escape   **Tony Oswick**

Retired civil servant Tony Oswick lives in Clacton-on-Sea and has been 'writing for pleasure' for 12 years. Although he tends to prefer more light-hearted or amusing subjects, occasionally he can be found writing serious stories.

The Right to Silence   **Angela Rozwadowski**

I live in the Cotswolds with my husband and have enjoyed writing short stories for several years. Only during lockdown did I consider entering competitions. I love the journeys my characters make – they stay with me long after the story ends.

Judgement Day   **Kevin Sleight**
A Barry boy (think Gavin and Stacey) now resident
just outside Bognor (don't forget the) Regis. Retired.
Nudging 70. Married. Two kids. Three grandkids. A few
goldfish. One-time civil servant (pin-stripe off, cardigan
on). Mathematician (but now more pie than pi). Avid
reader. Stephen King to Stephen Hawking.

Brandy Snap   **Jan Steer**
Jan loves to write. His short stories have been widely
published, winning many competitions. He has also
published a novel, *Someplace Else*. Some of his poems
have been published by Reach, Nine Muses, Sarasvati,
Dawn Treader and online. He lives peacefully in the
beautiful Welsh countryside.

Father Christmas   **David Stephens**
David Stephens is Professor of International Education
at the University of Brighton where he divides his
time between Brighton and Peru. His first novel, *Purely
Academic* (Arena Books), was published in 2017, and he
is now completing a collection of travel writing and *The
Disappeared*, a novel set in Peru.

Marty   **Andy Stewart**
Andy is a retired family doctor. He and his wife have a vineyard in Cornwall. He has penned satirical articles for medical journals under the guises of Dr Basil Bile and Dr Hugh Joverdraft, and enjoys writing short stories. He is halfway through giving birth to a humorous novel.

The Old Man in the Tree   **Maureen Taylor**
Maureen lives in the north-east of England. She came to creative writing fairly recently upon leaving full time work in criminal justice. She now appreciates being able to use language creatively to develop a character in their own world, along with the challenge of trying to tell this story in as few words as possible.

Room 304   **Ed Walsh**
Ed is a writer of novels and short stories. He is married and lives outside Durham, in the north-east. Recently shortlisted for the Lindisfarne Prize and seeking wider publication. Ed is pleased to be chosen for this Anthology and looks forward to reading the other inclusions.

Finale   **Steve Ward**

Steve Ward is a retired teacher with a PhD in Social History for his research into the history of the Circus. Since retiring, he has had ten books published, mostly to do with the circus, both commercially and self-published. *Finale* is his first venture into short story writing.

George's Lockdown   **Kurt Whelan**

After a lifetime working in the print industry as a graphic designer, at 64, I am now retired with time to pursue other interests: painting, photography, cycling and paddle-boarding. In 2016 I completed a degree with the Open University where I discovered the joy of creative writing.

That Was the Year   **Audrey Yeardley**

Looking back, down the long years, I took a very circuitous route but (as they say) a shifting landscape gives you different perspectives. So, by working on farms, running a remote inn, becoming an English teacher (and then becoming feral, with quite a lot of different jobs) here I am!